SPECIAL MESSAGE TO READERS

This book is published under the auspices of
THE ULVERSCROFT FOUNDATION
(registered charity No. 264873 UK)

Established in 1972 to provide funds for
research, diagnosis and treatment of eye diseases.
Examples of contributions made are: —

A new Children's Assessment Unit at
Moorfield's Hospital, London.

Twin operating theatres at the
Western Ophthalmic Hospital, London.

A Chair of Ophthalmology at the
University of Leicester.

The establishment of a Royal Australian College
of Ophthalmologists "Fellowship".

You can help further the work of the Foundation
by making a donation or leaving a legacy. Every
contribution, no matter how small, is received
with gratitude. Please write for details to:

THE ULVERSCROFT FOUNDATION,
The Green, Bradgate Road, Anstey,
Leicester LE7 7FU, England.
Telephone: (0116) 236 4325

In Australia write to:
THE ULVERSCROFT FOUNDATION,
c/o The Royal Australian College of
Ophthalmologists,
27, Commonwealth Street, Sydney,
N.S.W. 2010.

A WREATH OF POPPIES

To prove a case against one small-time Hong Kong dope-pusher seemed a simple enough task for the David Chan Detective Agency. Then came the doubts about the motives of a close-mouthed client. Suddenly Chan was too close to one of the giant Hong Kong narcotics syndicates, the knives were flashing among the sampans and a man dies violently aboard a blazing junk. The bland-faced Chan needs all his nimble wits and fighting skills just to stay alive.

CHARLES LEADER

◆

A WREATH OF POPPIES

Complete and Unabridged

LINFORD
Leicester

First published in Great Britain

First Linford Edition
published 1996

British Library CIP Data

Leader, Charles
    A wreath of poppies.—Large print ed.—
Linford mystery library
I. Title II. Series
823.914 [F]

    ISBN 0–7089–7862–2

Published by
F. A. Thorpe (Publishing) Ltd.
Anstey, Leicestershire

Set by Words & Graphics Ltd.
Anstey, Leicestershire
Printed and bound in Great Britain by
T. J. Press (Padstow) Ltd., Padstow, Cornwall

This book is printed on acid-free paper

1

"**MR. CHAN?**"
I paused with my hand on the doorknob and turned to face the owner of the soft, enquiring voice — and found myself looking directly into the cold, circular black hole that was the single nostril in the blunt nose of a Colt 0.45 automatic. This close the Colt looked like a cannon, and it was aimed at the point where my eyebrows might have met if they had formed a straight line. Behind the Colt was a big-knuckled fist and a hairy wrist disappearing into a crisp white shirt cuff that sported a heavy gold cufflink. Behind the gun and the fist and the cufflink was a hard, mangled face that had seen a lot of knuckle surgery in its time. It was the face of a losing boxer and not at all pleasing.

Old habits are hard to break, and I found myself wishing that my mother had not taught me to be truthful at all times. I nodded politely in answer to his question.

"Mr. David Chan?"

He was making quite sure, so I helped him by reading out the gilt-lettered words on the window of my office door.

" — Of the David Chan Detective Agency. Yes."

"Then you are the man that I want to see."

He eased back a little and lowered the Colt so that it was now aimed about a yard from my belly instead of a few inches from between my eyes. He was a big, heavy man of about forty-five, packed solidly into a grey suit. He was also a total stranger and I had no idea of what his business might be. He was watching me carefully.

I smiled at him blandly, mainly because I hate disappointing people, and I knew that most Westerners would expect an Oriental to respond with a bland smile.

"In that case," I said, "you had better come inside."

For a second his eyes showed uncertainty, as though the bland smile and calm acceptance of the situation wasn't quite what he had expected at all. However, I turned away without haste and completed the act of turning the doorknob, I pushed the door open and took two leisurely strides into the office, I didn't look back, but I kept my right hand on the edge of the door, and as I completed the second stride I slammed it violently behind me.

I heard his startled shout and the crash as the door knocked the Colt aside and smashed him in the face. I was still moving and in three fast strides I had reached my desk. I hit the desk top with the flat of my hand and vaulted over it, swivelling on the heel of my palm to land upright facing the door on the far side. With my right hand I flipped back the top drawer and picked up the 9mm Chinese automatic that lay inside.

I waited with the gun pointed at the half open door.

Although it was only three minutes past nine o'clock on a Monday morning my two partners had already arrived and were seated behind their desks on either side of the office. On my right Belinda had stopped with her fingers poised over the keys of her typewriter, and was gazing at me with an expression of mild curiosity through her spectacles. On my left Tracey had paused in the act of opening the morning mail, and she too showed a marked lack of surprise at my unusually acrobatic form of arrival. They had masterly facial control, enough to make the average unreadable Chinese look like an open book with capital exclamation marks.

After a moment they exchanged glances, shrugged almost imperceptibly, and then joined me in watching the door.

The door opened slowly, and the man with the Colt 0.45 came inside. It was a cautious entry and his gun hand was now hanging straight at his side with the weapon pointed innocently at the floor. He rubbed his bruised nose with the forefingers of his left hand and smiled ruefully.

"That was quite an exhibition, Mr. Chan." He seemed to think that the remark needed emphasis and so he added a repeat: "Quite an exhibition!"

"But why was it necessary?"

He looked uncomfortable. The Chinese automatic in my hand was something that he hadn't bargained for, and the cool, appraising stares that he was getting from Belinda and Tracey had him even more rattled. I had to admit, however, that those two girls were enough to disturb any sexually normal male. They were both stunningly beautiful, with vital statistics that were not only vital but practically fantastic. Tracey had red hair that fell about her shoulders like soft flames, while her eyes were the pure green of emeralds. Belinda was a perfect contrast, raven-haired, cool and poised, with liquid hazel eyes, even her elegant golden butterfly spectacles had sex appeal.

Our visitor remembered my question.

"I guess I was just checking you out, Mr. Chan," he said awkwardly. "You have such a high reputation here in Hong Kong that it made me curious. I just wanted to see if you could live up to it. I guess it was a stupid game to play — I'm sorry."

"It's dangerous to play games," I said softly. "The safety catch on that Colt 0.45 is off!"

"So is the safety on that piece of ironmongery you're holding!" he pointed out tartly.

I smiled my bland Oriental smile.

"But I'm not playing games!"

He looked angry for a moment, but there were two voices arguing in his mind and one of them was satisfied. He grinned and twiddled the Colt until he was holding it by the barrel, and then he advanced and laid it on the desk in front of me.

"It's empty," he said. "There's no magazine. You can check."

I did as he advised, and found that he was speaking the truth. I returned his Colt, and then put back the safety catch on the Chinese automatic and returned that to my desk drawer. He put the Colt in his jacket pocket. I closed the drawer of my desk and sat down. I decided that now I could afford to be hospitable.

"Tracey," I said. "Please bring a chair for our client." I looked up at our visitor. "I assume that you have come to this agency as a client?"

He nodded. "That's right. There's a job that I think you can do for me." He paused to thank Tracey and then sat down on the chair she had positioned behind him. "I'm still sorry about that dumb trick I pulled at the door," he continued. "It seemed like a good idea at the time, just to test your reaction. But now — "

"Forget it," I told him. "Let's make a fresh start. Who are you?"

"My name is Slater, Ralph Slater."

"An American?"

"That's right, from New York."

"Okay, Mr. Slater." I smiled at him as though we had now become close friends. "Tell me why you are here in Hong Kong? And why do you need a private detective?"

"Well, it's kinda — " He paused there, as if reluctant to go on. He didn't look round but I sensed that he was conscious of the two girls who were both waiting with interest.

"Let me introduce you to my partners," I said. "Miss Belinda Carrington is from England. She once worked for the International Council of Museums in Europe, until a financial crisis meant that they could no longer afford to pay her for the valuable work she was doing. Their loss was my gain, for Belinda is an art detective with an encyclopaedic knowledge in the field of art treasures and antiquities of all kinds. Tracking down art thieves and recovering stolen *objets d'art* was her speciality."

I paused while Slater turned in his chair and said hello to Belinda, and while Belinda said hello to Slater and gave him her demure smile.

"Miss Tracey Ryan is American," I continued. "Incidentally from your home town, New York. Tracey is another expert in her own field. She was for two years an agent of your Federal Bureau of Investigation, working on narcotics control."

Slater swung round quickly to look at Tracey, and there was something in the movement and in his eyes that I couldn't quite read. It might have been surprise, or pretended surprise, or even alarm.

Tracey said, "Hi!"

"Hi," Slater repeated, and there was uncertainty in his tone. I had to wait for him to look at me again, but by then he had his face and his voice under control.

"Tracey and Belinda are full partners," I repeated. "They supply the beauty and the brains, while I just own the office and do the occasional acrobatics." I gave him the bland smile treatment again. "So please, why have you come to see us?"

Slater gave me a hard look, and then decided that it was time to start explaining.

"I want you to bring a man to justice for me."

"Is he a criminal?"

"Too damn right he's a criminal. In fact criminal is too good a word for him, he's a crummy, low-down crook."

"Who is he, and what has he done?"

Slater fished inside his jacket and pulled out a leather wallet. From the wallet he took a photograph and pushed it across the desk. I picked it up. It was a blown up print of a young Chinese, but to me it meant nothing.

"His name is Lin Hoi," Slater said. "I want you to fix him — prove a case against him. I want to see him in jail."

"Let's start at the beginning," I suggested. "Why did you come to Hong Kong? And how did you meet this man Lin Hoi?"

"I haven't met him, not yet. I came to Hong Kong to find him." Slater paused there, and then decided on the best place to start. "I had a daughter, Mr. Chan. A nice kid, but a bit wild. Independent, determined to do her own thing. You know how even the best kids turn out these days?"

I nodded in sympathy. "What was her name?"

"Marion. That was her mother's name too, but her mother died when she was ten. I tried to bring her up right, but I didn't want to rule her. When she got through college she wanted to see a bit of the world while she was still young, the way

11

they all do these days. I didn't stop her. I don't know now if I could have stopped her, or even if I would have been right to try. She was twenty-one, old enough to know her own mind. I let her make this round-the-world trip she wanted."

"And in Hong Kong she met this man Lin Hoi," I said gently, trying to tie it all together.

Slater nodded. "She did the usual trip, through Afghanistan, India and Kathmandu. Maybe she started on hashish in some of those places, I don't know. I do know that she never touched any of that kind of stuff before she left the States. Anyway she moved on to Hong Kong. She stayed in some crummy hotel, and got mixed up with some bad company, young kids who were bumming around the world in much the same way as she was doing. They introduced her to this fellow Lin Hoi. He sold her some opium."

Slater had bunched each hand into

two big, hard-knuckled fists on my desk. He was getting himself worked up and his face was dark and angry.

"He sold her opium," he repeated. "A couple of times. And then the bastard persuaded her to try something stronger. He sold her heroin!"

"So Lin Hoi is a dope pusher," I said softly. I was beginning to understand, and my sympathy was becoming real.

"That's right." Slater stared down at his clenched fists as though he badly wanted to use them.

There was silence and I had to ask, "What happened next?"

"He made her an offer," Slater said harshly. "Her trip was almost over and she was leaving Hong Kong. He offered her one thousand US dollars to smuggle two three-ounce packets of pure heroin into the States and deliver them to a contact in New York. Six ounces of heroin sold at a grain a time for a fix will fetch over one-hundred-and-sixty thousand dollars on the New York black market, but my little girl didn't know that. She thought that smuggling two little packets for a crummy thousand was a good deal. They paid her five hundred at this end, and she got the other five hundred on delivery in New York. Her New York contact was so well satisfied that he gave her a bonus — a couple of free fixes of heroin!"

"And she got hooked?"

"That's right, Mr. Chan. That's how the bastards paid her off. They used her to smuggle dope, and then hooked her so that in time they even got back their crummy thousand when she had to buy more stuff."

"So now your daughter Marion is a confirmed drug addict?"

"Now my daughter Marion is dead," Slater said savagely. "All this happened twelve months ago. Three weeks ago she was fished out of the Hudson River. Whether she fell in accidentally while doped up, or whether she jumped in deliberately when she needed a fix and couldn't take any more doesn't really matter. She's dead, and it was heroin that killed her."

I leaned back in my chair and regarded him thoughtfully, giving him time to cool down.

"Let me just make sure that I've grasped the essential points," I said calmly. "Your daughter stayed in Hong Kong twelve months ago on a round the world trip. She was introduced to this man Lin Hoi who persuaded her to smuggle drugs into New York. Subsequently she got hooked and died. Now you want our agency to prove a case against Lin Hoi so that the police can take action. In effect you want revenge upon the man who caused your daughter to chase the dragon!"

"How do you mean, chase the dragon?"

"For the people involved narcotics is a business as well as a crime," Tracey Ryan informed him quietly. "Hong Kong is one of the world's major supply sources, and some of the bigger networks have their own hallmarks.

Dragon-triple-nine is the hallmark of best quality heroin, and so the Hong Kong teenager who gets hooked refers to himself as chasing the dragon. It's the local term for addiction."

"I see," Slater said slowly. He looked back to me. "You've got it right, Mr. Chan. What I want is for you to nail the man who started my daughter chasing the dragon!"

I nodded, but I was still puzzled. "There's just one mystery, Mr. Slater, why come to Hong Kong and pick on a cheap little pusher like Lin Hoi? I assume that your daughter must have talked to you before she died, otherwise you would not know as much as you have already told me. You know that she had contacts in New York, especially the man to whom she delivered the two packets she smuggled from Hong Kong — the man who gave her the heroin bonus! Surely he is the more evil person, and must bear the greatest responsibility for your daughter's sad death. It would be more

16

logical for you to make him the target for your revenge, and also you have the advantage that the man is resident on your doorstep. Why don't you take action in New York, instead of coming all this way to see me?"

"Because I don't know the name of her contact in New York," Slater said tartly. "Sure Marion talked to me before she died. She told me how she got started through this guy Lin Hoi. She seemed to figure that spilling names and places in Hong Kong didn't matter because it was all so far away. But she wouldn't say a damned word about the man who was still feeding her heroin in New York. She wouldn't give me his name, or tell me where to find him. She didn't want to jeopardize her source of supply. She wouldn't take that risk even with me."

He stopped, looking frustrated and angry again. Then he finished: "I haven't any positive leads in New York, but I do have one name here in Hong Kong. I'll settle for Lin Hoi

17

because he's the only real lead I've got, and he was the man who sold my Marion her first ever heroin fix. If I can nail him, then that at least will be something."

It sounded reasonable, so I looked at the photograph again.

"How did you get this picture?"

"I took it myself. Marion told me that Lin Hoi was a doorman at the *Jade Moon* nightclub in Tsimshatsui on Kowloon-side. So the first thing I did was to take a look at the club. I wasn't sure how to play it from there, so finally I just took a long distance telephoto shot of the doorman. Now I'm bringing it to you."

"So you can't be sure that this man is Lin Hoi! In twelve months the *Jade Moon* could have changed its doorman."

Slater looked embarrassed. "I didn't think of that."

"It doesn't matter now that you've come to us, if this isn't Lin Hoi I've no doubt that we can find him." I paused.

"Can you give the exact dates when your daughter stayed in Hong Kong?"

"It was April last year. She arrived at the beginning of the month on a French ship that came up from Bangkok. Then on the twenty-seventh she caught a Pan American flight back to the States."

I caught Belinda's eye and saw that she was quietly taking notes on her desk pad. "Where did Marion stay in Hong Kong?" I asked.

"Some place called Chungking Mansions in Kowloon."

I smiled. "I know it. It's a popular place for most young people passing through Hong Kong on the cheap. Do you know which room or apartment she had?"

"No, I don't." He was beginning to look annoyed.

"Do you have a photograph of Marion, Mr. Slater?"

"Well, no — I didn't think you'd — look I've given you the only photograph you need! What does it matter now what Marion looked like, she's dead and gone. Just nail the dope-peddling little bastard who sold her the goodbye kiss — that's all I want!"

He glared at me, but I retained my impassive Oriental calm.

"Mr. Slater," I told him gravely, "normally I would not touch a case in which the client was so clearly bent on revenge, but it so happens that I have as much distaste for men who trade in narcotics as you have. If you wish I will investigate this man Lin Hoi for you, and if he does prove to be a dope pusher I will try to bring him to justice. However, I am not a one-man band, and the services of this agency do not come cheaply. Our retainer is one hundred US dollars per day, plus expenses."

He didn't even blink. "I can pay it," he said. "I'll pay you a week in advance. But for this kind of money I expect results, and I expect to be kept fully informed of every step of the investigation. Is that a deal?"

I gazed into his hard grey eyes, trying to read what was hidden in his mind, but there were no clues. Finally I nodded.

"Okay, Mr. Slater. It's a deal."

2

AFTER Slater had answered a few more routine questions, and given us his telephone number and hotel address, he departed. I got up from my desk and wandered idly over to the window that looked down from the sixteenth floor of our office block. Immediately below was Connaught Road, and to the right was City Hall and the Star Ferry Pier. Directly opposite, across the junk and freighter scattered dazzle of the straights was Hong Kong's twin skyscraper city of Kowloon. I gazed at the view for a few moments to give Slater plenty of time to move away from the office door, and then turned back to my partners.

"Well, what do you think about Mr. Ralph Slater? Any comments?"

"There's something wrong," Tracey said bluntly. "I don't know what it is, but there was something about the way he looked at me when you told him that I worked for two years on narcotics control in New York. He looked startled almost uncertain — but why should that fact cause him any alarm?"

So Tracey had noticed that reaction too. Full marks for Tracey. I nodded wisely because at that moment I hadn't got an answer to her question, and then looked at Belinda.

"He was too vague about his daughter," Belinda said calmly. "And he didn't have a photograph. He's supposed to be a devoted father crying vengeance, but in his wallet he doesn't carry a single family snapshot he can show you."

I smiled, for they were expressing my own doubts exactly.

"You're two bright girls," I said.

Tracey nodded. "That's why this agency has been a success ever since we formed a team!"

"But you took the job, and Slater's

retainer," Belinda said, getting back to the point.

"At a hundred dollars a day I couldn't afford to turn it down, at least, not until we have a good and positive reason." I looked back to Tracey. "This is your field, you're our narcotics expert. So let's start with a refresher course on the current scene in Hong Kong."

Tracey nodded, and seated herself on the corner of her desk to oblige. There were times when I wished that she wouldn't do that, for she had lovely long legs and a very short skirt, and the combination made it difficult for me to concentrate and maintain a professional working relationship. I tried to take my eyes off the undercurve of her thigh, and keep my mind on the information I had requested.

"For a start Hong Kong is the major distribution centre for narcotics produced from the whole of South East Asia." Tracey had a solid bank of filing cabinets behind her, but for a general outline she could quote it all from memory. "The supply lines originate in the area that has become generally known as the golden triangle, that's the almost inaccessible hill regions of Burma, northern Thailand and Laos, and the southern Chinese province of Yunnan. There the local hill tribes grow huge fields of opium poppies. The seed pods are notched and the milky sap that runs out is dried and compressed into cakes of raw opium."

Tracey looked at me enquiringly to ensure that I was absorbing all this and I nodded. She continued:

"From the growing area the raw opium takes one of two routes. Either it gets smuggled south into Bangkok, and is then conveyed illicitly to Hong Kong by fishing boats; or it gets smuggled north through mainland China and across the border into the New Territories, or again it makes the final part of the journey by junk or sampan." She paused.

"There is even a rumour that the

supply pipeline in Yunnan is run by remnants of the old Nationalist Army who were cut off by the Communists when the bulk of that army retreated to Taiwan at the end of China's civil war. Those who were cut off hid their uniforms and turned to opium smuggling as their only alternative means of livelihood. They run the trade as a military operation, and if necessary use military force."

"And the Communists turn a blind eye?" Belinda asked.

"It seems so. The People's Government has banned Poppy cultivation, but they don't interfere with the trade that passes through to Hong Kong."

Belinda frowned. "So one way or another all the opium trails lead into Hong Kong?"

Tracey nodded. "Around Hong Kong and the New Territories there are thousands of bays, creeks and inlets, there are over eight thousand junks and God-alone knows how many sampans. The trade is impossible to stop. If you want figures then something like one and a half million US dollars gets spent every single day in this colony on drugs. There are a million addicts. And that's just the local picture. The bulk of the stuff gets refined into heroin and shipped out all over the world, but mostly to Europe and the States. Millions of air and sea travellers come and go every day, so that just makes distribution easier."

There was silence, and then Belinda gave me a stern look.

"Well, David Chan, it looks a pretty big picture! And just what do you propose that we should do about it?"

I loved Belinda when she fixed me with that sweetly sarcastic look. There was just the slightest pout about her full lips that made her look irresistibly kissable.

"Nothing," I said, restraining myself behind my bland expression. "All that I intend to do is to earn our fee and prove a case against one miserable little pusher."

"And how do you propose to do that?" Tracey asked.

"It's quite simple. If he is peddling dope, then all we have to do is to persuade him to sell some to us."

"And you really think that he will sell a couple of twists of heroin to you?"

"Not me," I acknowledged. "I couldn't possibly pretend to be another girl globetrotter who is a friend of Marion Slater and wants to try the same kick that she tried."

"You mean it has to be one of us," Belinda said coolly.

"I mean both of you," I said. "We do know that Lin Hoi prefers to get his hooks into young American girls travelling back to the States, but I wouldn't let Tracey go alone."

Tracey looked at Belinda and sighed. "Not only do we provide all the beauty and brains around here — he expects us to do all the work as well."

"I'll make the morning coffee," I conceded diplomatically.

★ ★ ★

The night life in Tsimshatsui started early, and so it was only eight-thirty in the evening when I boarded the Star Ferry to cross from Hong Kong island to the mainland city of Kowloon. I walked through the familiar neon-lit jungle of bar signs until I found the *Jade Moon*. A young Chinese in a bow tie and black tuxedo stood discreetly in the doorway, and I recognized the face from Slater's photograph. He did not bother to give me an invitation to come inside, or murmur the juicy praises of all the willing and available girls. That was reserved for servicemen and tourists. Instead he merely gave me a careless glance of indifference as I entered.

The bar was dimly lit, with the inevitable juke box flashing and shrieking like some science fiction horror in the corner. The customers were mostly American sailors and the bar girls were already at work, milking them of their dollars with the sweetest possible smiles. A couple of girls who were not yet occupied gave me doubtful glances, no doubt wondering whether I would be worth their time or whether it would be more profitable to wait until more sailors arrived. One of them yawned half-heartedly to suggest that she was bored and ready for company, and stretched lazily to extend her leg and reveal a few more inches of white thigh through the slit in her *cheongsam*. I refrained from smiling at her and she shrugged her shoulders as though it didn't really matter. I bought a beer and found myself an empty table by the door where I sipped it slowly pretending an idle interest in the background music.

After five minutes I shifted my position to gaze just as idly through the open doorway into the flickering, traffic-filled street. Five more minutes passed and then Tracey and Belinda appeared. Tracey wore a short emerald green dress that matched her eyes, while

Belinda wore an equally short dress of virgin white that contrasted with her raven black hair. They looked delicious, with a capital D.

They paused to hold a whispered conference, looking up briefly at the *Jade Moon* sign above the floor. Then they made a tentative approach. The interest of the young Chinese doorman was already aroused. His back was towards me, but I felt almost sure that he was licking his lips.

"Excuse me," I heard Tracey say uncertainly. "Is your name Lin Hoi?"

There was a moment of hesitation, as though the doorman had suddenly become wary, and then his head nodded slowly.

"Yes, that is my name. How did you know?"

"From a friend of mine," Tracey said. "A girl named Marion Slater. We were room-mates at college. I'm from New York, the same as Marion." She stopped there as though half afraid, and then asked, "You do remember

Marion, don't you?"

"Perhaps." Lin Hoi was refusing to commit himself.

"She was here about a year ago."

Lin Hoi shrugged cautiously. "There are so many American girls who pass through Hong Kong." He stared at her for a moment. "What is it that you want?"

Tracey glanced around nervously, and then lowered her voice. If I hadn't rehearsed her I wouldn't have known what she was saying.

"We want to buy some stuff. Marion told me that if I was ever in Hong Kong and wanted to smoke, then you could sell me the stuff."

Lin Hoi hesitated, and then looked at Belinda. "Who is your friend?"

"Just a friend. We met on the ship. We're travelling together."

"You are tourists from the *Manhattan Island*?" He named the giant American cruise liner that was berthed at Kowloon's Ocean Terminal.

Both girls nodded in answer.

Lin Hoi looked around nervously. I moved my gaze to look at the legs of the nearest bar girl just in time, and sipped my beer reflectively.

"You have money?" Lin Hoi asked softly. "You can pay ten US dollars?"

There was no answer, so I assume that Tracey merely nodded. There was silence, presumably while the girls waited and Lin Hoi debated in his own mind.

"Come back in an hour," he muttered at last. "I don't have the stuff with me. You must give me an hour."

I heard Tracey agreeing to the arrangement, and then she and Belinda moved away. Lin Hoi must have watched them depart, for a minute passed before he came into the bar and walked past me to the telephone that was situated in a glass booth in a corner behind the bar counter. I watched him dial, but his shoulder blocked my view and I couldn't get the number. At this stage of the game I didn't want to risk arousing his suspicions and scaring him off, so I resisted the temptation to drift up to the bar and listen in while I ordered another drink. Only the number would have been important anyway. I could imagine the conversation.

Lin Hoi talked urgently for two minutes, listened to his instructions, acknowledged, and then rang off.

★ ★ ★

At the end of the hour Tracey and Belinda returned. Lin Hoi was waiting and pulled them deeper into the shadows of the doorway. They went into a brief huddle with a minimum of whispered words and the transaction was made. Lin Hoi urged the two girls away as though eager to be rid of them, and I knew that Tracey was ten dollars poorer. This time it was all over in a hasty two minutes.

I waited long enough to allay any doubts, and then finished my beer and left. I returned to the office and found my two partners relaxing comfortably with a large gin and tonic each. The twist of paper that Tracey had purchased was waiting for me on my desk, lying open on my blotter to reveal a spoonful of white powder. Both girls smiled at me as I came in, and Tracey made a grand gesture with her hand.

"That's it, David — all of ten dollars worth."

I knew from the way she spoke that she had already tasted it, and that it was sweet and harmless. I dipped my finger into the powder and touched it to my tongue just to confirm. It was very pleasant, and taken by the ton would do no harm to anyone.

"Glucose," I said, with my most knowledgeable air.

Tracey nodded. "That's right, and as deadly as a bagful of candy!"

"But what did you expect?" Belinda asked, being practical as always.

"I expected a spoonful of glucose," I said calmly. "What else would a smart operator sell to a couple of naive young girls?"

They regarded me gravely, either marvelling at my masterly command of the situation, or deciding whether this was a fit moment for a combined assault upon my person.

"So we've had a wasted evening," Tracey observed. "What do you propose to do next?"

"I don't propose to do anything," I said. "I'm still leaving it all up to you. The *Manhattan Island* is stopping here for another four days, so your cover is still good. Tomorrow night you can go back to the *Jade Moon*. Tell Lin Hoi that although you tried to smoke some of his stuff, and although you tried injecting some, it just didn't give you any kicks. Tell him it wasn't good quality and you want something better. My guess is that if you act dumb enough, and keen enough, then he'll sell you the real stuff — at an inflated price."

"Keen and dumb!" Belinda said

acidly, and looked at Tracey for support.

"We can do it," Tracey said. "But we should get Oscars for our acting ability."

"I'll stand you each another gin and tonic," I consoled them.

★ ★ ★

It would have been too obvious for me to occupy the same table in the *Jade Moon* when Belinda and Tracey made their return visit, and so the following evening I installed myself in advance in the almost identical bar on the opposite side of the street. The clientele and the bar girls seemed the same, and only the name was different. I again found a table close to the door so that I could watch the doorway of the *Jade Moon* through the passing curtain of neon-lit faces and slowly cruising cars. Tracey and Belinda appeared on schedule and again tackled Lin Hoi.

This time I was too far away to

overhear, and the intervening traffic and the gossip of the pedestrians blotted out the low voices. However, I had again played the part of Lin Hoi during our afternoon rehearsals, and so I knew exactly what was being said. After a short conversation in the shadows of the doorway the two girls walked away, and I was not surprised to see Belinda raise her right hand and briefly rub her nose with her finger. It was the pre-arranged signal which meant that Lin Hoi had requested another one-hour delay, presumably to make another telephone call for instructions. I felt satisfied that we were getting somewhere, and ordered another beer.

Two beers later the sixty minutes were up, and I saw Tracey and Belinda reappear on the opposite side of the street. They stopped at the doorway of the *Jade Moon*, and this time Lin Hoi enticed them even deeper into the shadows. I watched, cursing the intervening traffic that persisted in partially blocking my view. They were talking in low voices but were not huddled as though a transaction was taking place. Minutes passed, and I realized that they were waiting for something to happen.

There was a movement of bright blue at one end of the street, and a very smart low-styled Porsche coupé slid smoothly into view. With scarcely a murmur of engine the car rolled to a stop outside the *Jade Moon*. Inside there was only the driver, a fat-faced, middle-aged and prosperous looking Chinese wearing plain-rimmed spectacles. He leaned over to open the passenger door, and over the top of the low, curved bonnet I saw Lin Hoi gently persuading my two girls to step forward.

Tracey and Belinda exchanged hesitant glances, then Tracey shrugged and got into the low blue car. Belinda ducked in behind her. The bespectacled driver was saying something reassuring and Lin Hoi closed the door behind them. With a low growl the blue car moved away.

I stepped out into the street, and with the blue car shielding me from Lin Hoi moved quickly along the pavement. As it drew level and then passed me I noted the registration number and committed it to my memory. It was all that I could do before the car accelerated and disappeared around the next corner.

It left me thwarted and very badly worried. Belinda Carrington and Tracey Ryan were two brave and capable young women, but they were playing an exceedingly dangerous game in an exceedingly dangerous city. Not for one moment had I intended to let them out of my sight and my protection, but already I had failed them.

3

I CAUGHT the Star Ferry back to Hong Kong and returned to my sixteenth floor office overlooking the harbour. By night the dark waters were ringed and sprinkled by a million glittering lights, and I had a view that could only be bettered from The Peak, but tonight I wasn't interested. I knew that the girls would call me as soon as they were able, and so I sat down behind my desk and watched the silent telephone. It was twenty minutes since I had walked away from the *Jade Moon*, and after another ten minutes had passed I opened my desk drawer and took out the 9mm Chinese automatic. I checked that the magazine was full and then laid the gun on the desk.

We Chinese are supposed to be inscrutable and unemotional, but that of course is just a Western fallacy. Threaten something or someone that we love and we react as fiercely as any other race. Also I was half English on my mother's side, and underneath my assumed bland smile there was bulldog blood in my veins. I suppose that if my father had been an English officer who had married a Chinese girl it would all have been considered rather sporting and jolly, and at the end of my public school education in England I might have stayed on to let the old school tie unlock the door to a respectable job. However, it hadn't worked out like that. My mother was a high spirited officer's daughter who had thrown every convention to the winds to marry a Chinese. My very existence had been frowned upon at my conservative English school, and so I had returned to Hong Kong to start a detective agency, I wasn't doing very well until I had the superb good fortune to meet up with Tracey and Belinda, but now we were a successful team.

More than that, I had an affection for them both.

Forty minutes was their deadline and I watched the second hand jerk round on my wristwatch. If the telephone did not ring within that time then I would make another journey to the *Jade Moon*, where Lin Hoi would tell me the name of the man in the blue car. He would also tell me where to find that man and where to find my two missing partners. He would tell me because the barrel of the Chinese automatic would be half way down his rotten throat and his only alternative would be to have the back of his head blown off. That's how inscrutable and unemotional we Chinese bulldogs can be!

The fortieth minute ticked past. I stood up, slipped off my jacket and pulled on the lightweight shoulder harness I kept with the gun. The automatic I dropped into the shoulder holster beneath my left armpit. I put my jacket on again, straightened it, and headed for the door.

Lin Hoi was saved by the bell.

I picked up the telephone and heard Belinda say blithely: "Hello, David. Don't press the panic button — we'll be home in half an hour."

"I knew there was nothing to worry about," I lied, and I heard her chuckle.

She rang off and I got out of my war gear and poured myself a small whisky.

They breezed in twenty-five minutes later looking well pleased with themselves. Tracey presented me with a small twist of silver paper which I carefully unwrapped to reveal a few grains of white powder. I knew automatically that this wasn't glucose.

"I think we hit jackpot," Tracey said.

I dipped a finger and brought it gently to the tip of my tongue. The taste was pungent and bitter and I immediately got up to rinse my mouth clean with a glass of water.

"You hit jackpot," I agreed. "Pure

heroin." I sat down again. "What happened?"

"We went for a ride with a nice little man in a blue car," Belinda said.

"I saw that much. Did he have a name?"

"He called himself Mr. Shing," Tracey took over the story. "He drove us to a car park where it was dark and quiet. I was all ready to get a half nelson round his sweet little neck when he stopped, but it was on the level and there was no one waiting. He asked us what we wanted, and we told him that the stuff Lin Hoi sold us didn't actually do anything and we wanted something stronger. He told us that what we had from Lin Hoi was poor quality opium. He was assuming that we wouldn't know opium from sherbet anyway. Then he said that he could sell us something really good, but that it would cost us fifty US dollars. He was a real con man! Anyway — we paid, and this is it." She grimaced. "As a special favour the little rat even told us how to take it."

"And that's all?" I was thinking that it could only have taken ten minutes and they had let me sweat for forty.

"Be patient, David," Belinda said severely. "Let Tracey finish."

"I told you we hit jackpot," Tracey continued with a smile. "So there's more. Mr. Shing began asking us a lot of questions, about the cruise ship we were supposed to be on, and when we were due back in the States. Also he wanted to know how I came to know about Lin Hoi. I told him how I was supposed to be a college friend of Marion Slater's and all that yarn. Anyway, after a lot of hedging he finally came up with an offer. It was the same offer that he made Marion Slater, a thousand dollars to take two packets back to New York."

It was better than I had dared to hope. "How did you play it?" I asked.

Tracey smiled. "I was supposed to be a naive female, remember? All I

46

could do was act in character, sort of half keen and half afraid, unable to make up my own mind. So he gave me until tomorrow night. I can think it over, and if I'm prepared to accept his offer then he'll meet us again outside the *Jade Moon* at the same time."

"I have the same option," Belinda added. "If I so decide then I can make a thousand dollars too."

"You're two smart girls," I said. "I love you both."

"Does that mean we're worth a rise?" Belinda asked hopefully.

"Not exactly, but it does mean that the office is prepared to stand another round of gin and tonics."

★ ★ ★

I telephoned Ralph Slater at nine o'clock the following morning, and by nine thirty he was in our office looking hard and eager and demanding a full report. I narrated the story of our progress to date, and then continued:

"I think that we're now in a position to wind this case up for you, Mr. Slater. And we'll throw in an extra service for the fee. Not only do we have enough evidence to convict Lin Hoi, but we can get this Mr. Shing for you as well."

"How do you plan it?" Slater asked.

"It's quite simple. Belinda and Tracey are prepared to meet Mr. Shing again to accept his offer. The deal is the same one that your daughter Marion had, five hundred at this end, and five hundred on delivery in New York. When my two partners are each handed five hundred dollars and two packets of heroin I shall be standing by with a few discreetly hidden officers of the Hong Kong police. The police can move in and arrest Shing red-handed."

I sat back and waited for the look of satisfaction to appear on Slater's face, but instead there slowly evolved an expression of doubt and uncertainty. I tried to read it but I was baffled. It could have been just doubt that the business could be concluded so easily, or perhaps this wasn't exactly what he had in mind. I couldn't be sure.

"I doubt if a small-time pusher like Lin Hoi would have more than one contact," I said at last, breaking the silence. "So it's reasonable to assume that Mr. Shing was also involved in the deal with Marion. If we can get convictions against these two men then we've done twice as much as you asked. Isn't that what you want?"

Slater looked startled. "Sure," he said, and smiled quickly. He swung round to face my two partners. "You girls have done a good job, and you took a lot of risks. I'm grateful for that. I really do appreciate it!"

He turned back to me and his smile faltered and he became doubtful again. "I was just thinking, Mr. Chan. You've really got a good line of investigation going. You've got one step higher than I expected you to get. Isn't it possible that if you keep going without bringing in the police, then we might get to the next man up in the line, the man above Mr. Shing?"

"No chance," I said flatly. "The Lin Hois and the Mr. Shings the police can round up any time. They're thicker than flies along the waterfront. But to get above the level of Mr. Shing is where the resources of every police force and narcotics agency in the world comes up against a blank wall. It's also the level where private pryers like myself can very quickly get killed. Mr. Shing is as far as I'm prepared to go."

He didn't like it, but he nodded reluctantly. "I suppose you're right, Mr. Chan. When are your girls meeting with Mr. Shing again."

"Tonight."

"And you'll bring in the police now?"

"Not yet," I said. "Mr. Shing is a long way from the top, but I doubt that he's a complete fool. He won't have any heroin with him tonight. He'll be wary of exactly the kind of trap we're planning, so he'll come clean and just ask the girls to confirm that they are willing to act as carriers. If they play it right, and if the whole business still feels right to Mr. Shing, then he'll make another appointment to make the actual transaction tomorrow night. It'll have to be tomorrow night, because the girls are playing the part of tourists on the *Manhattan Island*, and the ship sails for the States the following day."

"So tonight the two girls go it alone again?" Slater turned to look at Tracey and Belinda who sat behind their desks looking calm and beautiful.

"Not exactly," I said. "I won't deliberately take that kind of risk. Tonight I'll have my car in Kowloon and I'll keep my eye on them from a distance. There won't be hordes of police hanging round to scare our man off prematurely, but I shall be there if anything goes wrong."

"We've told him that it isn't necessary, Tracey said.

"After all, we are big girls now," Belinda added, "and we do know how

51

to take care of ourselves!"

"Just the same, he's right," Slater said. He swung back to me. "Mr. Chan, if you intend to follow them up in your car then it won't matter whether there's one man in that car or two. I want *in* on this! I want to come along!"

"It is not the policy of this agency to place a client in a position of possible danger," I said tactfully.

"To hell with that. Look, Mr. Chan — David" — he decided to get more friendly — "I didn't come to you because I'm some kind of nervous nellie who can't fight his fight. I came to you because I'm on strange territory and you have all the local know-how. But if there's a risk to these two young women and you feel that you ought to be there, then I want to be there too. I don't want a couple of pretty girls getting hurt for me!"

Belinda and Tracey looked suitably pleased with the compliments. Slater was adamant, and I knew it would be a long argument to talk him out of it. Also I wanted to get to know him better. I wanted to know what was in his mind.

"All right, Mr. Slater — ," I began.

"Ralph, David — call me Ralph."

"All right, Ralph, you can come along."

★ ★ ★

My car was a black Mercedes saloon, powerful and finely tuned, but not too ostentatious. When the time came I parked it about fifty yards back from the *Jade Moon*, trying to pick a spot where our faces would be in shadow despite the brilliant array of neon signs that dripped all the way along both sides of the narrow street. I had made one or two discreet attempts to pump our client, but so far all that I had got out of him was the vague admission that he was in the estate business. While we waited I struck up the conversation and tried again.

"You said you were in real estate, Ralph — does that mean that you buy and sell land?"

"Not land as much as property. I operate in New York, remember. Every square inch of land out there has already been developed." He gave me a strange look and seemed disinclined to talk about himself. "Tell me, David, how did you first meet up with those two luscious girls?"

"Belinda came out here on a holiday," I answered. "Three weeks in exotic Hong Kong. We met and I showed her around. At the end of her stay I offered her a job. She declined, but a year later her job with the International Council of Museums folded up, and she wrote to ask if my offer was still open. I automatically sent her an air ticket." I paused. "Is it your own business, Ralph, or part of a company?"

"My own business," he said. "But I'm not really big time. How did you meet Tracey?"

"I was introduced to her on a

business trip to San Francisco. Tracey did two years at law school and then four years with the FBI. She quit the service for personal reasons. She never did explain the details, so I would guess that it was a love affair that went wrong. She was at a loose end in San Francisco because it was the furthest point away from New York. When I offered her a job she grabbed it. She seems to find working with me less restrictive than being with the FBI." I paused again. "How long have you been in the estate business, Ralph?"

"Long enough," he said, and shrugged as though it was a subject not worth pursuing. "How about yourself, David? You're not all Chinese, are you? You're bigger than the average Chinese, and you look more European."

I smiled, because he was playing me at my own game and winning, maybe because I had nothing to hide. "My mother was English," I admitted. I didn't have to go any further because at that point Tracey and Belinda sauntered past on the pavement. We both became silent and watched as they reached the *Jade Moon*.

The two girls lingered in the bar doorway, where Lin Hoi greeted them like old and valued friends. They conversed for a few minutes, and then dead on time I saw the sleek blue Porsche sliding into view in my rear-view mirror. As it drew level only inches from my right shoulder I flicked my eyes right without turning my head. The blue Porsche was empty except for the driver, the same little fat-faced Chinese in the plain-rimmed spectacles.

The blue car stopped in front of the *Jade Moon*. Again Mr. Shing pushed open the passenger door and again Tracey and Belinda got inside. The doors closed and the car pulled smoothly away.

I started the engine, allowed another car to pass, and then eased the Mercedes into the traffic. Without making myself obvious I spared a glance for Lin Hoi, but the doorman was distracted by a couple of American sailors who had wandered along the pavement. He was trying to entice them inside the bar and saw nothing amiss. Satisfied I pressed my foot down and concentrated on keeping the blue Porsche in sight.

Mr. Shing made three sharp turns to regain the main Nathan Road that ran like a wide canyon of light, gaiety and dazzle down the centre of the long, peninsular city of Kowloon. Here the traffic was a dense flow, spaced out with big red British buses, but Mr. Shing drove at a sedate pace with no overtaking, which made him easy to follow. I could afford to play safe and allow a couple of vehicles to remain between us.

After five minutes the blue Porsche turned left along Jordan Road towards the car ferry. It was moving slowly and then turned left again along the unsavoury Canton road that ran behind the typhoon shelter and the waterfront. I assumed that Mr. Shing was conducting his business on the move, and so I held well back. I expected our quarry to make the full circle back into the bright lights and the *Jade Moon*, and so I knew that something was wrong when I saw the blue Porsche slowing right down to a stop.

I stopped the Mercedes a hundred yards back in a patch of shadow and waited. I saw the door of the blue Porsche open and Tracey and Belinda emerged uncertainly. Mr. Shing was leaning over, smiling and saying something reassuring, and then he closed the door and drove away.

"They're in trouble," I told Slater briefly. "He didn't dump them here for their health."

I slipped open the door and was already moving silently along the pavement when ahead the dark figures moved suddenly out of the shadows and converged upon the two girls in a violent rush.

4

THEY were six young thugs from the floating poverty of the packed sampans in the typhoon shelter, and here in this smelling, dim-lit backstreet behind the waterfront they were convinced that they had a clear field. I saw one of them sail over Belinda's right shoulder as she whipped his wrist and turned his flying body neatly over her hip. Another doubled over and dropped with a howl as Tracey's shapely toe speared him accurately in the lower abdomen. Then the two girls were buried under the combined onslaught of the rest of the gang.

I covered the last fifty yards in a racing sprint, ending in a long swallow dive that brought me crashing down on the melée of struggling bodies. I locked each arm around a startled neck, plucking an assailant away from each girl as I landed between them. I swung my body forward to brake on my heels, and then brought the two startled heads together and banged them hard. As the two men reeled away in a daze I dealt them each a savage hand chop across the back of the neck. I didn't pause to watch them fall but spun lightly on my heel.

Tracey was in the grip of a big, baffled Chinese who had suddenly realized that he ought to be facing me. As he released her and turned I sprang to meet him. I kicked him squarely in the crotch, an illegal version of Thai boxing, and as he doubled I axed him across the side of the neck with my stiffened palm. As my feet hit the pavement again I wheeled for a second time. The man Belinda had thrown was on his feet, but for good measure I delivered a straight right to his jaw that put him down again.

After that it was more or less all over. Slater was hammering the sixth man with some of the old-fashioned two-fist stuff, and Belinda was tidying her hair. Tracey smoothed the creases out of her green dress while I massaged the edge of my right hand.

"What went wrong?" I asked when we had all got our breath back.

"I've no idea," Tracey said wryly. "When we got into the car everything seemed to be going the way we had planned it. Mr. Shing was friendly, and when we told him that we had decided that we would do his smuggling job he looked pleased and beamed all over his fat little face. I asked him when would we get the packages he wanted us to smuggle, and the five hundred dollars advance. He said that he didn't have them with him tonight, he wanted to be sure first that we did want to do business. He said that he would meet us again tomorrow night to make the transaction before the *Manhattan Island* sailed from Hong Kong."

Slater had pummelled his man to the ground and now he came over to listen.

There was a dubious look on his face and he repeated my question.

"So what went wrong?"

"We don't know," Belinda said. "It all seemed to be going right until Mr. Shing stopped here. He was still polite and said that he had some more urgent business calls to make and that he was very sorry that he didn't have the time to take us back to the *Jade Moon*. He promised to meet us again tomorrow, but asked if we would mind walking back tonight."

"We knew it was going wrong," Tracey said, "but we also knew that you two were lurking about somewhere in David's car. It was worth taking a chance and pretending that we trusted him, just in case he was merely putting us to some kind of test to see whether we were really as dumb as we were supposed to be."

I frowned and thought. The girls waited for me to dispense some masterly flash of intuition, each with that slightly sardonic look which meant that they knew they were waiting in vain.

"Perhaps he tumbled to the fact that he was being followed," Slater suggested slowly.

"No." I was sure of that. "The girls weren't attacked by chance. This ambush was planned well ahead, which means that Shing knew they were feeding him a false yarn long before he picked them up outside the *Jade Moon*. Shing did some checking somewhere, and their story didn't hold up."

I looked back at the two girls. "He must have asked you for your names. What did you tell him?"

"We made up some false names," Belinda said. "I was Betty Smith, and Tracey was Sarah Brown. We thought that he just might have been able to link our real names with the David Chan Detective Agency."

"Good thinking, but it wasn't enough." I paused, and then said modestly, "Let's assume that Mr. Shing is as smart as I am. If I had doubts about a couple of girls who claimed to be tourists off a cruise ship in the harbour, then I'd find some way of checking the names they gave me against the ship's passenger list. My guess is that Mr. Shing did the same. When he found that there was no Betty Smith and no Sarah Brown listed among the *Manhattan Island*'s passengers, then he knew that he was being conned. So he decided to dump you here where you could be taught a lesson."

"So the whole thing's blown?" Slater said bitterly.

I nodded. "I'm sorry, Ralph. We were getting lucky, and it was all too good to be true. The best we can do now is to hand it all over to the police. Perhaps our Mr. Shing is on their records. The more they know the greater become their chances that they will eventually nail him down."

"But couldn't you find Mr. Shing again, without bringing in the police?"

I watched him carefully, wishing that

I could fathom what was in his mind.

"Perhaps," I admitted. "We know what he looks like, plus the description and registration number of his car. But what would be the point? Now that he's alert we could never hope to fix up another transaction and catch him in the act."

"Even so, I'd like to go on," Slater insisted. "I'd like you to go as far as we can before we bring in the law. That way I'd get some satisfaction. I'd feel that I did something personal to help make up for Marion! Can you understand that David? Will you try and find Shing for me?"

"I can understand," I said, although I didn't believe it. I nodded slowly, "Okay, Ralph, if you're prepared to keep paying, then we'll carry the investigation as far as we can."

Slater smiled, and looked relieved. Then for the first time he spared a thought for the gang of young toughs who had attacked the two girls. Half of them had already crawled away into the night, but the three remaining were still incapacitated and groaning.

"What about these guys?" he asked. "Do we hand them over to the police?"

I shook my head. "We let them go. They've had enough."

"But they attacked Tracey and Belinda!" He stared at me as though I was some kind of idiot.

I pointed down at the most lively of the three, who was trying to drag himself away with one hand clutching his bruised belly and a look of miserable fear in his eyes.

"Let me tell you about this guy," I said harshly. "He probably lives in a half-sinking sampan in the typhoon shelter back there. Maybe he's married and he's got a pregnant wife and a couple of starving babies he has to feed on a handful of rice. Or maybe he keeps his wife and babies in a doorway, or in a cupboard under the stairs in one of these crummy buildings. He's part of the Hong Kong population that the tourists are not encouraged to see! Sure he was prepared to rough up Tracey and Belinda, because he was paid for the job and that means a full rice bowl. If the price was right he might have killed them. But he didn't and we gave him a beating, and for me that's enough."

Slater said doubtfully, "There's a soft streak in you, David."

"No," I said. "I'm a harder bastard than any of them. That's why I'm standing on my feet and they're still down in the gutter. If a dog tries to bite me I'll kick it right in the teeth, but I don't kick it again when it's down."

"I guess you're right," Slater decided not to argue. "Maybe they have had enough."

We watched the object of our discussion get to his feet and stumble away at a lurching run, but there were still two of his friends on the pavement. Looking at them and looking at Slater a devious thought crossed my mind.

"There's something you might consider," I said conversationally. "This gang would work for you just as readily as they worked for Mr. Shing. You came here to fix Lin Hoi, and if you really want him fixed then they would do it permanently. It would cost you less than you're paying our agency, and you could fly home tomorrow!"

Slater gave me another long stare, and I didn't know whether he was weighing up the idea or trying to read my mind in turn. Then he shook his head.

"That's all Lin Hoi deserves, but I'd rather not do it that way. I'd like it better if you can get another lead on to Mr. Shing."

I hadn't read anything useful out of his reaction so I shrugged. "Okay, Ralph, we'll start tomorrow. Now let's go back to the car."

★ ★ ★

Tracey and Belinda were waiting expectantly at the office when I arrived five minutes late the following morning, both of them looking keen, calm and collected.

"Well," Tracey asked, "Where do you want us to start?"

"Not with Mr. Shing," I said positively. "From now on I'll handle that end of the investigation." They looked ready to mutiny so I hastily explained what I expected from them. "You two girls can take an easy day. Just wander around Chungking mansions, and find out whether any of the longer term residents can remember an American girl named Marion Slater?"

"What's the angle?" Belinda wanted to know.

"Just this, last night you two could have got killed, because Mr. Shing knew you were spinning him a yarn. I suggested that Mr. Shing could have checked the passenger list of the *Manhattan Island*, and perhaps he did. But there's another possibility I didn't like to mention in front of Ralph Slater, and that's the possibility that you went to Mr. Shing with false references. You told him that you were friends of Marion Slater, but I'm beginning to wonder whether there ever was a girl named Marion Slater — and if there was whether she ever did come to Hong Kong?"

Belinda looked thoughtfully at Tracey.

"It's a good question," Tracey conceded.

They collected their handbags and headed for the door.

★ ★ ★

I spent the day tracking down the blue Porsche coupé. German made cars were not exactly plentiful in the Colony, and this one was a brand new model. I tried the listed Porsche dealers first but drew a blank and had to cast my net wider. I could have short-cut by using the telephone, but I preferred to make a personal approach which made it a long job. After the first few garages and showrooms I evolved a routine, which was simply to express an interest in buying a new coupé for myself, and then dropping hints that I had seen a smart blue model of the exact car that I wanted cruising around Kowloon. When that approach failed it was time to enquire more directly whether such a car had been sold in the past twelve months, weighing up the attendant or salesman at the same time, and if necessary hinting at a bribe for the right information.

It sounds easy, but it meant a lot of weary leg-work, and in Kowloon I drew a blank. I returned to Hong Kong-side and finally hit the right garage about mid-afternoon. A sharp little sales clerk pricked up his ears and admitted that perhaps they had sold a blue Porsche coupé of the type that interested me. It would be several months ago and he couldn't be sure.

I slipped my wallet out of the inside pocket of my jacket and opened it, ostensibly to withdraw a slip of white card, but in fact to let him see that

71

I was not exactly poor. I gave him the card.

"This is the registration number of the car I saw in Kowloon," I said blandly. "Perhaps you could check in your books and find out whether it was the same car you sold here."

He smiled. "It would not be difficult, sir. But it would be most irregular for me to reveal details of one customer to another."

"Of course," I nodded my understanding. "And I would not ask you to commit an irregularity for nothing." I offered him two HK five dollar bills.

He hesitated, and then took the notes and put them in his shirt pocket. Then he pulled a large ledger across the counter and checked the registration number I had given him against the numbers of the cars that had been sold. After flipping back half a dozen pages he stopped.

"Yes, sir," he said brightly. "This garage did sell this car."

We gazed at each other with satisfied

smiles, and after a minute I opened my wallet again. Five HK dollars were worth a fraction less than one US dollar, and Slater was paying my expenses anyway. I gave him two more notes.

"This will buy the name and address of the man who bought the blue Porsche car," I told him firmly.

He nodded cheerfully. "This car was purchased by a man named Mr. Shing, who lives at apartment number two-three-nine in Paradise Building on Hong Kong." He turned the ledger so that I could check the written entry and verify his honesty.

I made a note of the address, thanked the sales clerk and gave him another bill to keep him sweet. We parted friends.

* * *

I returned to my black Mercedes and drove over to Paradise Building. It was a large, white skyscraper block of luxury flats rising up against the blue sky and the green shoulder of the Peak. Beneath the block was an underground car park for residents only. I surveyed the scene and then drove back across Hong Kong to make a brief call at the office. I collected my camera, fitted it with a film and a telescopic lens, and then returned to the car, and ultimately to Paradise Building. I parked in the street within long-range shooting distance of the ramp that descended into the underground car park, and there I waited.

The hours passed slowly. A few smart and expensive cars passed up and down the ramp, but no blue Porsche coupé. I felt a temptation to go to sleep.

At six o'clock came the rush hour. Traffic filled the streets as the shops and offices closed. The inhabitants of Paradise Building began to return in greater numbers. I waited for another hour until the rush died down again, and then my patience was rewarded. I saw the blue Porsche coupé approach and slow down to turn into the underground garage.

The camera was ready on the seat beside me, and I lifted it into position. I had already focussed it for light and distance, and as the blue car turned on to the ramp I saw the familiar fat face and spectacles of Mr. Shing at the wheel. The telephoto lens brought him quite close and I clicked the camera. I wound the film quickly, adjusted the exposure fractionally, and got one more shot for luck before the face of Mr. Shing and his blue car passed out of sight.

I took the camera along to a small photographers shop in Des Voeux Road where the proprietor was a personal friend of mine. The film was developed while I waited, and in less than an hour I had a couple of fairly clear profile prints of the face of Mr. Shing. I took those along to Sunny's gymnasium.

I was well known at the gym, for I usually managed to put in at least an hour there each day, limbering up on the parallel bars, practising a few judo throws, or keeping up to the mark with my Thai boxing. I couldn't afford to be anything but physically fit, and the gym was well run and well equipped. It was owned by Sun Cheong, a deceptively fat Chinese with a permanent smile, who was known to all his close acquaintances as Sunny. Despite his weight and shape he was fast and agile, and could hold his own on the mats with most of his customers. Also he was another close friend who frequently gave me a helping hand in a variety of ways. If I needed some extra weight I could always rely on Sunny, and inevitably there would be a bunch of idle young athletes practising around the gym whom he could employ in turn.

After the usual greetings and banter

about his waistline I showed Sunny the photograph of Mr. Shing in his blue car.

"I want him followed," I said. "When he leaves Paradise Building tomorrow morning I want to know where he goes and what he does. I want to know what his business is. I want to know who he meets and who his friends are. I want to know everything about him. It will be a two or three man job to keep watch on him for a few days. Will you help me?"

"With pleasure," Sunny smiled and the laughter creases spread across his fat face. "It has not been a very interesting week, and some of our friends are bored. You know we will enjoy helping you."

"He deals in heroin," I warned. "So don't get too close. I don't want anyone to get hurt."

The smile hardened on Sunny's face. "I do not like heroin dealers," he said slowly. "This one I will watch myself."

"Keep me informed," I said, "and if there's any risk — pull out."

I briefed him with all I had on Mr. Shing and he listened carefully. Afterwards I changed into shorts and running shoes, and went through my daily routine on the ropes and bars.

5

SUNNY was as good as his word, and I received a telephone call from him in the middle of the following morning. He sounded moderately pleased with himself as he made his first report.

"Hello, David? I think that I have found out a little more for you. I waited outside Paradise Building this morning until the blue car left with our friend inside. He was alone and drove down to the vehicular ferry pier. I had my own car and followed him on board. We crossed the straights to Kowloon-side. I was able to continue following him when he drove off the ferry into Jordan Road. I am now telephoning from Man Lung Road, which is in one of the industrial and resettlement areas on the way out to the New Territories. Mr. Shing has parked his car and disappeared into the premises of the Happy Valley Fruit Company."

"That sounds like progress," I said appreciatively. "Will you stand by until I arrive?"

"Sure thing, David. You will find my car parked at the south end of Man Lung Road. I shall appear to be asleep inside."

I thanked him and rang off. It took me three minutes to locate Man Lung Road on the map, it was in the middle of the sprawl of shabby streets shoved well back behind the bright facade of Kowloon. The girls had not yet arrived, so I left them a note on my desk, collected my car keys and departed.

The journey took less than an hour. The ferry ride was a pleasure, for the sky was blue with a white froth of clouds, and it was impossible to tire of the magnificent scenery of the harbour, ringed with white skyscrapers and dotted with fishing junks and the anchored freighters from every port in the world. Also the trip with the car ferry to Jordan Road was satisfyingly longer than the short, five-minute haul on the Star Ferry which was for passengers only. The rest of the hour was taken up with the drive through the back streets of Kowloon, a bustling maze hung with vertical chinese shop signs and crowded with people and traffic to the point of frustration. It seemed that every street was competing with its neighbour in packing in the maximum number of cars and faces and boldly splashed banners of Chinese characters.

Eventually I came in sight of the giant tenement blocks that were Hong Kong's attempted answer to its chronic over-population and lack of housing. Grey, drab, square and massive, they were draped by millions of waving shirts, socks and underpants stuck out of the windows on washing poles to dry. Grossly overcrowded in their turn, they were made cheerful only by the bustle and the indefatigable smiles of the swarms of Chinese who lived there. I turned away from them, searching through an area of shoddy business premises and sweat-shop factories until I found Man Lung Road.

Sunny owned an ancient white Pontiac. It had been a smart car in its time, but it was a bit too wide for the narrower streets of Hong Kong and Kowloon, and over the years had collected enough bumps and dents and scratches to give it a well-battered appearance. When I spotted it I drove past and parked my own car in the next street. I didn't want some smart observer noticing the two cars parked together, and so I chose to walk back to the Pontiac. I opened the passenger door and slid inside.

Sunny was leaning back in the driving seat with his hands clasped complacently over his generous stomach. His white hat was pulled over his eyes but after a moment he lifted his head to let it tilt back. His round face smiled.

"You're a ham," I told him. "Every

private eye you've ever seen on the American movies does that."

"Sure," he chuckled. "Every guy who sees me thinks — there's a funny fat guy, pretending like he's a movie private eye. Then they laugh and forget about me. They don't take me seriously."

"I hope you're right," I said doubtfully.

Sunny's face retained its confident beam. He had no doubts at all. He pointed down the row of paint-peeling, banner-draped buildings to the sign that read HAPPY VALLEY FRUIT COMPANY, both in English and Chinese.

"Our mutual friend Mr. Shing is still inside," he informed me. "At the side of the building is a narrow alley where he has parked the blue Porsche car. As far as I can determine without making myself obvious the Happy Valley Fruit Company manufacturers plastic fruits."

I gazed thoughtfully down the street. "I'll scout around," I said at last. "You wait here."

He nodded and settled back into his position of repose. I got out of the car and walked slowly down the street. The pre-noon sun was hot on my shoulders, and the dust and scraps of waste paper stirred listlessly in the gutters. There was less hubbub and movement than in the crowded shopping streets further back, but there were still enough pedestrians on the pavements to make me just one of a passing stream. I didn't linger outside the open doorway of the Happy Valley Fruit Company, but I did notice that even the girl clerk was perspiring at her reception desk. Obviously the company didn't believe in wasting its money on any cooling ventilation, and I could only guess at the conditions of the hidden workers. Like the employees of every other company in this area they undoubtedly worked long hours for low wages, and made fat profits for the rich Chinese businessmen who lived remotely on the upper slopes of The Peak.

I walked on, past the mouth of the side alley that was only just wide enough to take the sleek blue Porsche coupé. On the opposite side of the street was a small Chinese restaurant with chickens, bunches of tomatoes and onions and plates of rice and peppers prominently displayed in a glass case. I walked another hundred yards and then crossed the road and walked back to the restaurant. I went inside and took a seat at an empty table by the open door.

It was still too early for a meal, so I simply ordered tea and a couple of chinese cakes, light, fluffy pastry with a spiral of white sugar on top. Business was slack and the young Chinese who served me was in no hurry. I looked across the road and admired the blue Porsche coupé.

"That is a very nice car," I said. as I paid for the tea and cakes. "I should very much like to own a car like that."

The waiter looked and nodded. "Very nice," he agreed. "It will travel at over one hundred miles per hour. I could get many girls if I had such a car!"

"Then it is not your car?"

He laughed at the joke. "No, I am too poor to own a car like that. The car belongs to Mr. Shing."

I took a bite from my cake. "This Mr. Shing must be a very important man to own a car like that," I said conversationally.

Again the waiter nodded. "Mr. Shing is the owner of the Happy Valley Fruit Company. He exports fruit that no one can eat to all over the world. Isn't that crazy?"

He showed me a bowl of display fruits that stood in the window, which were presumably the produce of the Happy Valley Fruit Company. There were a couple of plastic oranges, plastic apples, a plastic banana and a plastic pear. They looked colourful and almost real.

"Mr. Shing is not so crazy if he can sell these and make enough money to buy the blue car," I said pointedly.

"And the blue car must get Mr. Shing many girls."

My informant shrugged critically. "Perhaps, but most of the time the blue car just stands there. Mr. Shing comes to the factory most mornings at nine o'clock, and does not leave until six in the evening," He grinned. "If I were Mr. Shing I would spend less time at the factory and more time with the girls."

"Perhaps that is why you are not Mr. Shing, and do not own a factory and a blue car," I suggested.

We laughed together, and then he moved away to greet another customer while I finished my tea and cakes.

I eventually returned to Sunny and the white Pontiac and told him the little I had learned. It seemed unlikely that Mr. Shing would leave the factory during working hours, but we couldn't be sure and I wanted the watch maintained. I wanted to know what other connections Mr. Shing might have. Sunny had to be back on Hong

Kong-side in the early afternoon to open up the gym, but he had already arranged for a relief from among his trusted circle of young regulars. I was satisfied with the arrangements and left him a couple of hundred HK dollars to cover his expenses and payments to anyone else whose time he employed. The rest we would settle up later.

While Sunny waited for his relief I picked up my Mercedes and drove back through Kowloon. For the sake of convenience I decided to leave the car in an underground park and took the Star Ferry back to Hong Kong.

★ ★ ★

When I walked into my office my two partners were already there. It was too early for gin and tonics so they were making coffee. Belinda wore a short, pencil-slim skirt in blue and yellow check, with blue high heels and a yellow silk blouse, while Tracey wore gold slacks and a pale green shirt to heighten her flame red hair. They both looked adorable, cool and competent as always.

"Hi, there!" They said in chorus.

"Hi," I answered. "I thought you girls had married a couple of millionaires and deserted me."

"No, sir," Tracey said. "Life with some creaking old millionaire would be just too dull. We've been working."

"We called in last night, but you were out," Belinda added.

"I work here too," I reminded them. "What did you find out?"

Tracey shrugged. "We drew a blank. We checked out Chungking Mansions. It's part of a big block off Nathan Road in Kowloon that's let out as cheap hotel rooms. Mostly the people who stay there are European or American travellers passing through on a low budget. They're mostly young, and usually they only stay for a few weeks. There were a few long-term Chinese residents, but they don't remember a girl called Marion Slater. The people

89

who own and staff the place don't remember her either, but that doesn't really prove anything." She smiled wryly. "The Chinese claim that all American girls look the same, and there have been quite a few of them staying at Chungking Mansions at one time or another."

"Don't they keep books?"

"Sure, but half the entries are illegible. No one can positively say that Marion Slater did stay there, and no one can positively say that she didn't."

"All we can positively say," Belinda concluded helpfully, "is that if Marion Slater did stop off in Hong Kong in April last year, then Chungking Mansions is the most likely place that she might have stayed!"

"Great," I said. "That brings us neatly back to square one. What else have you been doing to pass the time?"

They both smiled, which meant that I couldn't accuse them of being idle.

"We thought that we'd do a little

checking on Ralph Slater himself," Belinda said. "We found out that although he is supposed to be a stranger with no contacts in Hong Kong, he has made several long telephone calls since his arrival, and on two occasions he's been absent from his hotel until the early hours of the morning. On each of those occasions he's returned stone cold sober without a single hair or a trace of face powder on his coat sleeve — which seems to suggest that he hasn't been having fun and games in the night clubs."

I gazed at them with admiration. "How did you learn all that?" I asked.

"From the girl receptionist at his hotel," Belinda explained nonchalantly. "We have our hair set at the same salon, so I do know her slightly. I pretended that I had a passing fancy for Mr. Slater, and I wondered what he would be like. She gave me her considered opinion, plus what little she actually knew about him. It was girl-to-girl stuff." Belinda gave me a frank look that was direct and reproving, and indicated that I would be impolite to the point of rudeness if I asked for any further details.

"There's something odd about our client," Tracey said, tactfully dismissing the delicate subject of their methods. "I can't pin it down, but each time I see him I get the persistent feeling that I've seen him somewhere before."

I looked into her emerald green eyes, but they couldn't tell me what she didn't yet know herself.

"You took a long time to mention it," I said slowly.

She nodded. "I know. When we first met I thought that it was just the sharp way he looked at me that struck a wrong note. But there was something more. It's such a vague feeling that I tried to reject it, but it keeps coming back every time I think of him and picture his face."

"You come from New York," I said. "Slater comes from New York. Maybe you saw him in a bar once, or a restaurant. Maybe you both stood face to face on a crowded subway and never even spoke!"

"Maybe," she said doubtfully. "But that kind of encounter wouldn't register at all." She screwed her face up into a frown, and then relaxed and shrugged. "Perhaps I'm imagining things, and if not it will come in its own good time."

I nodded and let it drop. I couldn't help her, and she couldn't force an amorphous doubt into something positive. We could only wait until it crystalized.

"What about you, David?" Belinda enquired. "How have you been frittering your time away?"

I told them how and where I had located Mr. Shing, and they did me the honour of looking suitably impressed. When I had finished my tale we were silent and thoughtful for a moment, and then Tracey posed a question.

"You said that Mr. Shing exports his plastic fruits to all parts of the world.

93

Obviously they won't be solid plastic, they'll be hollow, and that means that they would make ideal containers for smuggling heroin. We know that Mr. Shing does deal in heroin, but the fact that he also owns the Happy Valley Fruit Company could mean that he's a much bigger fish than we realized. It is possible that he's part of one of the big syndicates?"

"That thought did cross my mind," I admitted. "But for the moment we don't know."

"So how do we find out?" Belinda was always practical.

"For the moment we mark time," I said. "We have to give Sunny and his boys a couple of days to keep Mr. Shing under continuous observation. Then we take note of the way the case develops."

"What about Ralph Slater?" Tracey asked.

"We'll keep a discreet eye on his movements too just for the record."

★ ★ ★

That night and all the following day there was nothing from Sunny except routine telephone reports. It seemed that Mr. Shing was doing nothing more exciting than travelling to and fro between his home and his place of work. Sunny and his helpers were keeping a record of the descriptions of all visitors to the Happy Valley Fruit Company, but so far the period of observation was too short to start separating the regular from the casual callers.

Ralph Slater was also doing nothing to arouse suspicion. He called for a progress report each day, but I stalled him into believing that we were still searching for the blue coupé.

Then, late on the second night, events began to move. I was relaxing in my bachelor apartment with a scotch and a new psychological novel, and it was nearly midnight when I closed the book. I took a shower and prepared for bed, but while I was still brushing my teeth the telephone rang. I picked it up and heard the familiar voice of Sunny at the other end.

"Hello, David. I think that I am again on to something that might interest you. Mr. Shing did not return to Hong Kong and Paradise Building tonight. Instead he spent the evening at an apartment block in Kowloon. He left there an hour ago and drove out to Castle Peak Bay in the New Territories. Do you know the place?"

"I know it," I said. It was one of the bigger bays with a massed junk and sampan population.

"Mr. Shing has gone on board one of the larger fishing junks," Sunny concluded.

"Stay there and wait for me," I said briefly. "I'll be there as quickly as I can."

6

MY car was still parked on Kowloon-side and so I took the Star Ferry back across the Straits. For a few brief minutes it was like being afloat on some multi-coloured fairyland lake between islands of massed neon stars. By night the harbour and the twin cities created one vast, exotic Aladdin's Cave of jewelled lights. I picked up my car and drove fast up the equally fantastic dazzle of Nathan Road, but then the brilliance faded behind me as I headed out into the hills of the New Territories.

I passed the great square rabbit warrens of the tenement blocks, and then the big modern factories, textile firms and weaving and dyeing mills that were the prelude to the small industrial town of Tsuen Wan. After Tsuen Wan the road followed the twists and turns of the deeply indented coastline. On my left was the dark sea, with the occasional flicker of light that marked a lone junk, and on my right the hidden rice fields that were so much a part of the old China. The night was very black with no moon and few stars, a totally different world to the bright city I had left behind. The road was empty and I was able to put my foot down hard.

Castle Peak was one of the biggest bays on the westward side of the New Territories. It was another natural haven for junks and sampans that were packed so tight in the inner waters that there was barely room to float a match-box between them. The slanted masts of the fishing junks were like corn stubble thrusting out of a water-born rubbish heap of hulls and ropes and canvas. Behind the bay, which was speckled with lights, was the vast rising bulk of Castle Peak itself. Once a beacon had flashed from the highest point of the peak to warn the pearling fleets of approaching pirates, but those days were past and now the hill was in total darkness.

I drove the Mercedes slowly along the one road through the ramshackle shanty-town of shops and cafes that lined the waterfront. There were few lights and fewer people, but in a patch of shadow I found the battered white hulk of Sunny's old Pontiac. I pulled in behind it and got out to investigate. The Pontiac was locked and empty. There was no sign of Sunny.

Castle Peak was only a twenty mile drive from Kowloon, but due to the delay in crossing the Straits and the initial traffic jams in the city it was now almost an hour since Sunny had telephoned. I began to wonder what had happened in that hour.

I walked slowly back along the road towards the mouth of the bay. One solitary old man in faded blue jacket and trousers and a boatman's wide straw hat went past, giving me a brief but uninterested look. Otherwise

I was alone. Through the gaps in the buildings on my right I could just distinguish the slant of masts and the isolated flicker of a paraffin lamp. The smell of the sea, salt and fish was strong on the cool night air. I could sense the unseen presence of the thousands of human beings lying asleep or sleepless on the cramped deckboards of the crowded sampans. As I walked I listened, and I searched the darkness and the shadows. My senses were all alert, and when I finally heard the muffled sound from my right I swung to face it.

"Hello, David," Sunny said, and chuckled softly at the fright he had given me.

I stepped off the street and into the black mouth of the alleyway where he waited. I could just determine the pale, smiling moon of his face, and behind him another low outline that was also faintly familiar. I touched a curving slope of polished steel, and realized that my hand was resting on the blue

Porsche coupé that belonged to Mr. Shing.

"I watched your car go past," Sunny said quietly, "But I didn't want to break the watch. I knew you would spot the Pontiac and then walk up and down to look for me."

"What's been happening?" I asked.

"Since I telephoned you, nothing. Mr. Shing is still on board the junk."

He signed me to follow him and squeezed past the Porsche coupé that all but blocked the alleyway. His shirt front snagged for a moment on the car's door handle while his buttocks were pressed up tight against the wooden wall of the nearest building. He struggled to get free and then I followed him through with less difficulty. Underfoot something squelched and I smelled rotten fruit. Sunny guided me through the short alleyway which ultimately led on to an equally narrow wooden jetty that stuck out like a rotten finger into the bay.

Here at the mouth of the bay the

solid mass of sampans was broken up into individual craft. They lay silent on the black sheet of still water, with behind them the looming silhouette of Castle Peak. Sunny pointed out one of the largest and more isolated junks which was riding at anchor without lights.

"That is the craft. A sampan took Mr. Shing across, but then returned without him. I have kept a careful watch ever since, but there has been no more sign of movement."

I stared dubiously at the junk and the bay. There was only one way to discover what kind of business Mr. Shing was conducting out there at this ungodly hour of the night, and that was to go out there myself and eavesdrop. To take a sampan as Mr. Shing had done was out of the question. There would be no sampans left unattended, and although no sampan owner would ever complain at being woken up to earn a few dollars, regardless of the hour of the day or night, none of them could be relied upon to do the job in silence, or to refrain from talking afterwards. There was only one other way of getting out there, and very reluctantly I began to take off my jacket and shoes.

"I'm going out there to take a look," I said quietly.

"Rather you than me," Sunny said with feeling, although I knew that swimming was one of his favourite sports, and that he had no aversion to practising it in more savoury waters.

I gave him my surplus clothing and then climbed down over the end of the jetty. I eased my body slowly into the cold water, for the whole exercise would be pointless if I were to cause enough splashing to wake the sleeping bodies in the nearest sampans. Sunny looked down at me as I submerged to my shoulders, and I saw his face screw up into a grimace of revulsion. It was a feeling I shared but I let go the supports of the jetty and turned to swim silently out into the bay. Deeper inland I would not have entered the water for a million dollars, but here in the mouth of the bay the tides kept the water moving and comparatively clean. Even so I swam with my head high and my mouth shut. I had no desire to swallow a mouthful of instant typhoid.

The junk that Sunny had pointed out to me lay about a hundred yards out in the bay. It was a sixty-foot deep-sea vessel with a high, square stern, and as I swam closer I was able to read the chinese characters painted crudely along the slope of her blunt bows. She had been christened the *Fragrant Lotus* and belonged to the Cheng-Weng Junk Company registered in Hong Kong. I allowed the tide to carry me silently against her hull, and there reached up to hook my fingers into a loop of fishing net that was spilling untidily over the side.

I listened but heard nothing, and after a minute I slowly began to pull myself up. I transferred my grip to the edge of the hull and pulled my body clear of the water until I could see over the cluttered deck. There was a careless jumble of nets and old ropes, cork floats and a pile of wickerwork lobster baskets. Those and the smell were enough to tell me that the junk was used for deep-sea fishing.

I looked towards the high stern that housed the cabins. Now I could see that there was a dim glimmer of light inside, behind the drawn curtains of the windows, and also there was a low mutter of voices. They were speaking Cantonese, but although I knew the language I was not yet close enough to distinguish the muffled words.

I decided to play safe and check out the rest of the craft before making any serious attempt to listen in at the cabin window. I wanted to be sure that there were no stray crew members who might suddenly appear behind me. Very carefully I drew my legs out of the sea and eased myself silently over the gunwale and down on to the deck. The pile of nets screened me from the high poop deck and I moved swiftly but silently over to the raised cargo hatch that was open to the black night sky. I listened but I could hear no sound of breathing below.

I hesitated for a moment, wondering whether it would be worth the time and effort to make a closer investigation of the hold. If the *Fragrant Lotus* carried only fish then she was innocent and I was wasting my time here, but if she ran alternative cargoes then there might be traces of something other than dead fish scales down in the black bowels of the ship. That thought decided me, for I had to acknowledge that Mr. Shing had already had over an hour undisturbed to conclude his business, and that the tail end of his conversation might do little to repay me for risking my health in the foul waters of the bay. I swung my legs into the open hatchway, found a rope ladder dangling beneath me, and quickly descended into the stygian darkness.

At the bottom I paused, listening again, but all that I could hear was the gentle slap of the low waves on the outside of the junk's hull. After a moment I was satisfied that I was alone and reached into the top pocket of my shirt for the small torch that I habitually carried on any nocturnal enterprise. The torch was the size of a fountain pen and I hooded the narrow beam with my hand as I played it slowly around the hold.

There was nothing except more of the same items that littered the deck above; more nets, and more ropes, and more lobster and crab baskets. In one corner was a stack of empty fish boxes, and everything stank of fish scales and dead fish. So far the junk smelled and looked just the way any ordinary fishing junk would smell and look, and the suspect presence of Mr. Shing was the only incriminating point against it.

I began to move around the hold and examine it in more detail. I disturbed a rat which scuttled squeaking out of the range of my torch beam, but there was nothing else alive. I moved several of the fish boxes, scrutinizing each box in turn, but they all reeked of nothing but fish. I played the torch over the floor and the inside of the hold itself, looking for something — anything — that might have got caught between the multiple cracks and joints between the ribs and planking. In the far corner of the hold my patience was finally rewarded. The torch beam settled on a small white pile of fish scales that had accumulated against a rib, and when I disturbed the pile with my toe I kicked out a broken portion of flat round cake that had been buried and overlooked. I picked it up. It was almost black in colour and had the soft texture of putty. Tracey was my narcotics expert, but I didn't need her to tell me that what I was holding now was a small chunk of raw opium.

I dropped the small piece of opium cake into the top pocket of my shirt and buttoned the flap. It was evidence that the *Fragrant Lotus* had made at least one smuggling trip, and that established another link in the narcotics chain. I could learn nothing more here, and my thoughts turned to that muffled conversation in the poop deck cabin once again. I began to make my way back to the rope ladder that led up to the hatchway, but then something touched a warning nerve and I stopped.

I froze for a moment. It wasn't a sound that I had heard, nor the hint of another presence, yet I knew instinctively that something was wrong. Five seconds passed before I realized what it was. The junk was moving, drifting slowly and silently out towards the open sea.

Two points were obvious: one, even though the junk was drifting on the outgoing tide, it could not have moved unless some human hand had quietly shipped the anchor; and two, if she was making an innocent voyage in the normal way then the normal method would have been to start the auxiliary motor to help her steer clear of the cluttered shipping. Into those two facts I read an ominous conclusion. My own presence on board had been detected, and the crew had cast off and allowed the junk to drift so that I could be dealt with more effectively out of sight and sound of the shore. They had refrained from starting the engine because that would have alarmed me too soon.

I hesitated, but there was a third point that was equally obvious. Even if my conclusions were correct there was still only one way out of the junk's hold. Whether there was a reception committee or not I had to ascend the rope ladder through the hatchway to find out. I switched off my torch and looked up at the square patch of lesser darkness above. The junk was shrouded in silence but beginning to pitch slightly into the rising waves. I put the torch in my pocket and slowly began to climb. My heart was beating fast but my head was cool.

My hands reached the topmost rung of the ladder. I hung there in the darkness below the hatchway and carefully brought my feet up as high as possible so that my body was bunched in a tight ball. I could still hear nothing, but the very silence convinced me that there must be a reception committee. I flexed my muscles, rocked my body gently to swing the rope ladder, and then on the upward swing I launched myself upwards with one almighty heave.

They were waiting for me to raise my slow, foolish head very cautiously above the level of the hatchway, and then all three of them would have competed in the great joke of kicking my slow, foolish head from my slow, foolish shoulders. What they didn't expect was for me to catapult abruptly out of the hatchway like an erect jack-in-the-box, and I finished my momentum with a violent head butt that caught the man immediately facing me square in the belly. As he bowled over backwards with a loud and startled grunt I hung on and allowed his weight to pull me clear of the hatch. Then I rolled desperately to one side.

The other two were younger and faster than their collapsed shipmate, two supple young Chinese who had clearly learned how to skip about the moving decks of their craft in the odd typhoon. Their initial surprise gave me perhaps two seconds before they reacted, but then they were upon me like two tiger cats. One wielded a knife and the other a short-handled axe.

As the knife-boy sprang I swung both feet up to meet him. The heels of my feet slammed hard into his crotch and lifted him twelve inches higher than he had intended. Instead of landing on my chest with the knife poised to strike he passed clean over the top of me and crashed down heavily on the deck. His friend with the axe took a murderous swipe at my head, but again I rolled and the blow missed, the axe blade biting deep into the deck planking. As I struggled up my left hand caught a tangle of nets and I hurled them over the axe-boy's head.

I was on my feet only just in time. A fourth man had appeared at the head of the gangway ladder leading to the upper poop deck. He carried a lighted paraffin lamp which threw a dancing yellow light over the scene, and when he saw that the first three crew members were already down he let out a roar of rage and charged straight at me. He wasn't thinking clearly because he swung the burning oil lamp in a wild blow that was aimed for the side of my head. I ducked and drove a fist into his belly. The lamp sailed out of his hand and smashed on the edge of the gunwale, scattering broken glass and blazing paraffin over a heap of sun-baked nets. The nets and the whole port side of the junk burst merrily into a blaze of flames.

I turned ready to dive over the side, but the man I had butted as I burst out of the hatchway had regained his feet and caught me in a sudden bear hold. He was a big man with sheer bull strength that exceeded my own, and with his arms locked around my waist from behind I was trapped. We reeled drunkenly across the deck as I tried to twist and use my elbows, but for the moment I couldn't break his hold. Then the knife-boy came at me again, lunging for my lower abdomen. I twisted away frantically and the blade missed my hip by a fraction and stabbed into the man behind me. He released me with his howl of pain. As he staggered back I smashed him in the face with my left elbow, his heels hit the raised structure of the hatchway, and he howled again as he toppled backwards into the hold. The knife-boy looked startled at the mistake he had inadvertently made, and taking advantage of that I hooked a right cross to his jaw that sent him spinning out of the picture. His friend with the axe had rallied for another charge, but this time I was poised on my feet to face him. I caught the descending axe-wrist with both hands, half turned low to slam my right shoulder against the lower part of his chest, and then completed a routine throw that broke his right arm and pitched him over the junk's side into the sea.

I looked around for the fourth man, but for him one try was enough. He followed his friend voluntarily over the side without any further help from me.

The flames were now roaring high, eating deeply into the weathered and sun-bleached timbers. Within a few minutes the junk would be a furnace and it was time for me too to abandon ship. However, for the moment I held back. The four men who had attacked me all had the appearance of being the junk's crew, but there was a fifth man who should have put in an appearance.

I wondered what had happened to Mr. Shing.

Sunny had said that Mr. Shing was on board, and during my tour of the hold I had heard no slap of oars to indicate that his sampan had returned to take him away. I had time to satisfy my curiosity and ran quickly to check the cabins in the high stern. Within ten seconds I found the answer to all my questions, for Mr. Shing lay very neatly upon his back on the floor of the main cabin. The fat face wore an expression of faint surprise, and his eyes were glazed behind his plain-rimmed spectacles. His arms were neatly folded below the hilt of the knife that still protruded from his chest, and beneath him some thoughtful soul had carefully placed some old newspapers to ensure that his blood did not stain the deckboards before he was dumped.

There was nothing that I could do for a dead Mr. Shing, and so I left him and ran back on deck. The flames licked hungrily at my face and I wasted no more time in diving over the side and back into the murky black waters of the bay.

I began to swim swiftly away from the *Fragrant Lotus*, which was now blazing up into a quite spectacular pillar of fire.

7

"**G**OOD morning David."

Belinda and Tracey entered the office together like a well rehearsed double-act. If they had worn swimsuits instead of their gay print dresses they could have doubled for Miss England and Miss America giving a final and insoluble headache to a battery of judges with the thankless task of deciding which of them should be Miss World. They looked as bright and fresh as a couple of springtime daisies, and I waited anxiously to see whether they would wrinkle up their pretty noses as they came closer. They didn't, and so I concluded with relief that the hour I had spent in the bath last night had removed all traces of my nocturnal swim in Castle Peak Bay.

"Good morning," I said.

"What's new?" Belinda wanted to

know, and so I showed them the meagre result of my search in the hold of the *Fragrant Lotus*.

Tracey picked up the small portion of flattened black cake and now she did wrinkle her nose with distaste.

"Raw opium," she confirmed, "straight from the poppy fields. You could smoke it, if you wanted to dope yourself into a stupefied dream world, or — if you really wanted to rot your brain and end up screaming — you could refine it to extract the pure heroin."

"I don't intend to do either," I assured her.

"Where did you get it?" Belinda asked.

I gave them a detailed account of my adventures of the previous night, including my discovery of the late and unlamented Mr. Shing. They listened in serious silence, and finally Belinda said quietly:

"We're getting very deep into this David. It started out as an investigation into a small-time pusher, and now

119

we're manoeuvring close to one of the big drug syndicates and a man has been murdered. For a small agency we could be getting out of our depth."

"I agree," I said. "But Mr. Shing is literally a dead end now. We could tell Slater that, and be justified in handing the whole case over to the police."

"Is that what you intend to do?" Tracey asked.

I smiled wryly. "Perhaps, but my curiosity has been aroused on several points, and I don't really relish the idea of handing over a job that's only half finished. At least I'll talk to Slater before I decide."

"And what do you want us to do in the meantime?"

"Nothing," I said. "It gets dangerous in the deep end. There are big sharks with fearsome teeth. I'd prefer you girls to stay out of it."

"Some hope!" Tracey said. "We're full partners, remember, not mere employees. And anyway, who would take care of you?"

"I don't need — "

"Even without Mr. Shing there are still two lines of investigation we can follow," Belinda interrupted me calmly. "One is the Happy Valley Fruit Company, and the other is the Cheng-Weng Junk Company."

"You are not — "

"Does that young Superintendent still fancy you?" Tracey was also ignoring me and addressing Belinda.

"You mean Ray Davies?" Belinda nodded. "He makes a polite pass every time we meet."

"He could be worth pumping," Tracey said. "We know he works on narcotics control, and mostly with sea-born traffic. If the police know or suspect anything about the Cheng-Weng junks then he will know the facts."

"Chief Superintendent Ray Davies is a very smart policeman," I warned them. "You won't fool him for a minute."

"We don't want to make a fool of

him," Tracey answered. "We merely want to extract a little information from him. And we are two very smart girls."

"He usually has a lunch-time drink in the *Ship Inn* on Kowloon-side," Belinda said thoughtfully. "It's the nearest place in Hong Kong to a British pub, he feels at home there. We could just happen to be there when he comes in."

Having decided between themselves they turned to me again.

"We can't come to any harm talking to an English policeman," Tracey said.

Belinda smiled. "Actually we could if we accused him of being English. He's a Welshman, which is something quite different."

I gazed at them both severely. "You've convinced me." I said. "As long as you don't make any other investigations I shall permit you to go ahead."

In the circumstances there was very little else that I could say.

122

★ ★ ★

I called on Ralph Slater at his hotel, deciding that this time I would catch him on his own ground. A muffled voice answered my knock, shouting that the door was open. I presumed that he meant that the door was unlocked, and took it as an invitation to open the door and go inside. It was an ordinary hotel room in an ordinary hotel, and almost immediately Slater emerged from the bathroom. He was only just up and had only just shaved. He finished drying his rough-hewn face and threw the towel behind him. He was suddenly alert.

"Hi, David. Have you brought me some news?"

"Some," I admitted. "I've found Mr. Shing for you."

"Hey, that's just great. Who is he? Where is he? No, wait!" He raised a hand and grinned. "Let's be civilized. I'll pour you a cup of coffee, and then you tell me."

There was a breakfast tray with

silver coffee pot and a single cup and saucer standing on a side table. Obviously the tray had been delivered only moments before my arrival, and I tried to decline the only cup. Slater insisted and American hospitality won the day. I let him pour me a cup of coffee, and then he found a toothglass which he filled carefully for himself. We sat down, myself on a chair and Slater on the edge of the unmade bed. He sipped his coffee and continuously passed the hot glass from hand to hand. He grinned again.

"Well, David — give!"

"Mr. Shing has an apartment in one of the big new blocks on Hong Kong," I said calmly. "The block is called Paradise Building, and the apartment is number two-three-nine. We've also learned that Mr. Shing is a business man, and that he owns a small factory in Man Lung Road in Kowloon. It's a place called the Happy Valley Fruit Company. It's a sweat shop that manufactures plastic display fruits, mainly for export."

"Plastic display fruits," Slater repeated thoughtfully. "That kind of product would be an ideal cover for smuggling heroin."

I nodded. He was as sharp as Tracey, and I watched him with my face composed into a suitable bland expression.

"How did you get on to all this?" He demanded.

"We traced the blue Porsche coupé. For a man in his profession Mr. Shing should have chosen a more common make of car."

"Good work," Slater said approvingly. He swapped the hot glass of coffee from hand to hand again. "So what comes next, David? Can you keep watch on Shing and find out anymore."

I shook my head. "Not a chance. Mr. Shing isn't going to lead us any further. Last night a friend of mine followed Mr. Shing out to a junk harbour in the New Territories. When I got there I found Mr. Shing still on

125

board one of the junks. Mr. Shing was dead. Somebody had knifed him, and no doubt he would have been quietly deposited at sea if I had not disturbed things a little." I paused and then concluded casually. "The junk caught fire."

Slater was staring at me. "You say that you found him dead! Who killed him — and why?"

"I don't know who killed him," I admitted. "But I can guess at why he was killed. Somebody knew that Mr. Shing had been exposed. Somebody knew that my agency was keeping him under observation, and that we were getting too close to matters that we had no business to know. Therefore Mr. Shing became a danger to the men above him, and therefore Mr. Shing had to be eliminated. It was the safest course of action. Now the trail is cold. Mr. Shing was our only lead and Mr. Shing is no longer here to lead us. The bigger fish in the syndicate that employed him can now relax again."

Slater was still staring at me, and now either his coffee had cooled or he had forgotten that the hot glass was burning his hand. We were back at the old game of trying to read each others minds.

"But we're not right out of leads, are we?" he said slowly. "We still have this plastic fruit company to follow up. And what about this junk where you found Mr. Shing? It must have owners, or at least a skipper, maybe they tie up somewhere."

"The *Fragrant Lotus* was owned by the Cheng-Weng Junk Company," I said quietly. "And it has made at least one drug-running trip. Before I found Mr. Shing I also found this in the hold." I showed him what I had found.

"Raw opium," Slater said, recognizing the portion of flat, black cake as quickly and as positively as Tracey had done before him. He looked up with a glint of excitement in his eye. "You know what this means, David? If that junk company is smuggling raw opium into Hong Kong, and if Mr. Shing was smuggling the pure heroin out inside his plastic apples and grapes, then we only have to find the final link and we can wrap this whole operation up!"

There were two unproven ifs in his hypothesis, but for the moment I ignored them. "What is this final link?" I asked blandly.

"Damn it, David — the factory! The place where they refine the raw opium into heroin."

"Of course, there must be a factory," I tried to sound abashed, but then I looked at him hard. "Ralph, just what did you have in mind when you came to me? You asked me to tackle one small-time pusher, but now I'm mixing my weight with a whole big-time syndicate. How far do you expect me to go?"

"As far as you can." Slater paused, and tried to look apologetic. "I came to you straight, David. I wanted Lin Hoi because he was the only name I had, and the only part of this business I ever hoped to find. But now that we've really started to open up this case he just doesn't matter any more. At the start it would have been enough to put Lin Hoi in jail. That would have been something for Marion. But now I can see that I can do so much better than that. For Marion's sake I want to bust open as much of this syndicate as we can. If we can locate that final link then we've got the whole chain."

"From here on it gets dangerous," I said bluntly. "They've killed once and they'll kill again. I don't particularly want to end up like Mr. Shing."

"I'll double your retainer!"

"It's even more dangerous than that."

"Then I'll treble it!" He had no hesitation about it. "I'll pay you three hundred US dollars a day to continue this investigation as far as you can."

I pretended to think it over, and finally I nodded.

"Okay, Ralph, for that price I'll do it."

"I was sure you would," He smiled. "But one thing still stands, David. I want to be kept informed. So far I don't think that you've been communicating as fast as you could communicate. From here on I want to know every step as you make it. Because when it gets hot I want to be on hand to help you out. I told you before, I'm not afraid to fight my fight. I need your local knowledge, but if it comes to it I can pitch in my own muscle."

I returned his smile in a friendly manner. "You're paying the money, Ralph, so you call the tune!"

★ ★ ★

I had to visit Sunny to square up our accounts, and to assure him that I would not hesitate to call on his services if I needed him again. Then to work up an appetite for lunch I spent an hour on the parallel bars. It was afternoon when I finally got back to

130

the office and I found that Belinda and Tracey had also returned. Belinda was applying fresh lipstick, while Tracey was idly reading a newspaper.

"Well," I said sternly. "Did you two vamps succeed in seducing that innocent and unsuspecting policeman?"

"We didn't have to seduce him," Belinda replied calmly. "We simply allowed him to buy us a gin and tonic each, and then made conversation."

"And what did you converse about?"

"This among other things."

Tracey showed me the paper she was reading, and in the bottom left hand corner I saw the brief headline JUNK ABLAZE AT CASTLE PEAK. The story added that the junk *Fragrant Lotus* had come adrift from her moorings and then caught fire in the early hours of the morning. The craft had sunk in deep water and salvage was not considered worthwhile. Three of the four-man crew had escaped to report that a paraffin lamp had been knocked over accidentally. The fourth man, the junk skipper, was presumed to have drowned.

I handed the paper back without comment. The missing skipper could only be the big man I had toppled into the hold. There was no mention of Mr. Shing who had also found a watery grave, but I had not expected that there would be.

"That report made it easy," Belinda said, "We were reading it when Ray came in. We passed casual comment, and he remarked that it would be no great loss if all of the Cheng-Weng junks went the same way. We looked interested so he explained. The Cheng-Weng Junk Company runs six more large fishing junks about the same size as the *Fragrant Lotus*, and they've all been suspected of smuggling opium for a very long time. The trouble is that despite a number of spot checks the junks are always clean. The cargo is always fish."

"What keeps the police suspicious is that the catch is always too small to warrant the length of time the junks spend at sea," Tracey continued. "Yet the Chung-Weng Junk Company still makes money and thrives. Superintendent Davies is convinced that the company must be involved in drug smuggling, but the junk skippers are all too clever to get caught in the act."

They regarded me in silence, and then Belinda concluded, "Well, isn't that what you wanted to know."

I nodded. "It's exactly what I wanted to know."

"So what did you learn from Slater?"

"I learned that he wants us to push on with this case as far as we can. And he's now paying us three hundred US dollars per day to do it." I paused and then added slowly. "I also learned that Mr. Slater is quite knowledgeable on the subject of narcotics. He can recognize raw opium as readily as anyone here, and he knows the sequence of processes for refining opium into heroin. He wants us to find the heroin factory."

"He wants a lot," Tracey said. "And for an estate agent on his first trip to Hong Kong he knows too much."

I nodded.

"But we're still on the case?" Belinda said.

"I'm still on the case! You girls — "

"David," they said together, "please don't start getting tiresome again. You know you're not a solo agent any more."

I would have argued, but at that moment the doorbell rang. My face must have expressed frustration, for Belinda gave me a consoling smile while Tracey moved to answer the door. She opened it to admit a young Chinese woman who stood nervously on the threshold.

"I am looking for Mr. Chan," our visitor said hesitantly.

Tracey invited her in and I stood up behind my desk. Before I had been out-numbered but I suddenly felt overwhelmed as I faced the new arrival. She had long-lashed, almond-shaped eyes in a delicate white face, while her glossy black hair was drawn back smoothly into a short pony tail. Her body was perfection poured into a wine-red *cheongsam*, the high collar fitting neatly round her slender white throat, and the long skirt slit to show four inches of superb thigh above her knee. I felt as though Miss China had suddenly made her entry into the Miss World contest around me.

"I am David Chan," I conceded with as much composure as I could muster. "Can I help you?"

"Please, yes. My name is May Ling. I am hoping that you can perhaps — " she paused discreetly.

Belinda and Tracey had already collected their handbags.

"Please excuse us," Belinda said. "We were just on our way out."

"We have some calls to make," Tracey added, and she gave me a sly and unbecoming wink over Miss China's shoulder.

They disappeared together and left me to find our visitor a chair. When we were both seated I smiled reassuringly.

"Now," I said, "let us start again. How can I help you?"

"I want to find a missing person," she said, regarding me with wide candid, eyes. "Do you do this sort of work?"

I nodded. "We do get many such requests, and sometimes we are successful. Who is the missing person that you want us to find?"

"He is a good friend of mine," she answered demurely. "His name is Mr. Shing and he is the owner of the Happy Valley Fruit Company."

8

MY Chinese instinct came to the fore, and for perhaps three seconds I sat completely motionless with the traditional inscrutable face. Then the moment of surprise was past and inwardly I relaxed. My expression did not change and my eyes still held her own, and I wondered if she could possibly be as innocent as I pretended to be. We continued to smile blandly at each other.

"This Mr. Shing," I said calmly, "is he a relative of yours?"

"No," she moved her head in a slight negative gesture, and succeeded in looking mildly embarrassed. "As I have told you, Mr. Shing is just a close friend — a gentleman friend."

The emphasis she placed on the word 'gentleman' indicated a friendship of an amorous nature, and as I too was a gentleman I tactfully passed it by until such a time when we might become better acquainted.

"When did you last see your friend?" I enquired.

"It was last night, he came to my apartment. He stayed for a few hours and then left at about eleven o'clock. I expected him to telephone me this morning, but he did not ring. So I telephoned his place of work, the Happy Valley Fruit Company. His chief clerk told me that he was expected there today, but that they have not seen him. I telephoned his home to find out if he was ill, but he was not there. I am worried, and so I have come to you."

"But isn't it a little early to engage the services of a private detective? You say that you saw your friend only last night. Today perhaps he is taking a holiday, visiting more friends, or relatives perhaps?"

May Ling shook her head. "No, he had no other close friends, and no relatives."

"A sudden business call perhaps?"

"If he had planned a business trip he would have told me so last night. Or if something had come up unexpectedly he would have telephoned me."

"Then you were very close friends?"

She hesitated over the implication, and looked down at her hands clasped demurely in her lap. Finally she nodded.

"Yes — we were close friends. This morning I went to his apartment after I had telephoned the Happy Valley Fruit Company. Mr. Shing has an apartment here on Hong Kong-side in Paradise Building. I — I have a key. Mr. Shing was not there, and his car was not in the garage beneath the building. His neighbours told me that they did not hear Mr. Shing come home last night." She looked up at me with appealing eyes. "I feel very much that something bad has happened to him."

"Have you any reason for this fear? Does your Mr. Shing have enemies?"

She became vague. "Not enemies

exactly, but I think that he may have debts. Mr. Shing likes very much to gamble. Sometimes he bets much money. I think he could be in trouble this way."

"I see." I made that sound as though I considered her sense of logic perfectly acceptable. "But why come to me? Why haven't you gone to the police?"

She paused, and then looked at me almost sadly, giving me the whole wistful benefit of those seductive, tear-sweetened eyes.

"I felt that the police would be too — too impersonal. That is why I came to you, Mr. Chan. The police are so busy that I feel they would not spare too much of their time to look for Mr. Shing. I think that you will be more considerate and helpful."

"Thank you for the compliment." I smiled and then added with a note of regret. "But I am afraid that you will also find me more expensive."

"What is your fee?"

I considered. "If I accept this case

I shall have to charge you one hundred HK dollars per day. You must appreciate that I do not work alone, and that you will be employing the services of the agency."

"I understand," she said calmly. "I can pay."

We gazed candidly into each others eyes and it was my turn to smile.

"Then I accept the case. I will do what I can to find Mr. Shing for you. Perhaps you can tell me some more about his gambling debts? Where does he gamble? And to whom does he owe money?"

She looked uncomfortable. "I do not know. These are things that he does not tell me. I think that sometimes he goes to the casinos, and sometimes he plays dice and cards at private parties."

"Where are these private parties held?"

"Again I do not know. I am sorry."

She looked as though she was indeed sorry, a poor, helpless little girl lost, pleading for the comfort of my strong male arm. Her eyes looked as though they might brim up with tears at any moment.

I said gently. "Then where would you suggest that I start my investigation?"

"I thought," she said hesitantly, "that perhaps we might talk to the people at the Happy Valley Fruit Company. Or perhaps we might go to Mr. Shing's apartment in Paradise Building. Perhaps somewhere we shall find some clue?"

I smiled at her yet again. In my book golden opportunities were like coincidences, as rare as one-thousand-year old Chinese eggs, and even then they usually had the same none-too-subtle aroma. I knew that I was going to waste my time, but while I was being paid double I could afford to play along.

"I suppose they would be the logical places to start," I agreed. "Shall we go now?"

She smiled gratefully, and blinked

those lovely liquid eyes.

"If you wish, Mr. Chan — I am ready."

★ ★ ★

Three quarters of an hour later we were cruising slowly down Man Lung Road. I stopped the black Mercedes outside the familiar facade of the Happy Valley Fruit Company, and turned with an expression of innocent enquiry to May Ling who sat by my side. She nodded seriously, and acknowledged that this was the right place. I switched off the engine and we got out of the car.

May Ling preceded me up the two dusty steps into the reception office. She was obviously known there as a trusted friend of the missing owner, for she introduced me in turn to the girl clerk, and then the chief clerk, and finally to the factory manager. I talked to them all, making professional notes of their names and addresses, and I went through the painstaking routine of asking them all the same set of questions. How long had they worked for Mr. Shing? Was he a good employer who was liked and respected by his workers? What was their own relationship with Mr. Shing? Did he give any of them any hint that he expected to be absent from his home and work for a few days? Did they know whether he gambled, and where he gambled, and how often? Did they know whether Mr. Shing had any debts or business worries?

Their answers all fitted neatly into one set pattern. Mr. Shing was an average employer who was neither especially liked or disliked by his workers. He was, it was suggested, no better and no worse than any other Chinese businessman. All those questioned insisted that their own relationships with Mr. Shing were good but formal. They worked together well enough, but he was their employer and they did not mix socially. Mr. Shing was a man of habit who worked hard and expected his employees to work harder. Normally he spent all working hours at the factory, unless he was engaged upon business meetings with prospective buyers. If he expected to be absent he always informed the chief clerk, but yesterday he had given no indication that today would not be a normal working day. Nobody could suggest any explanation for his disappearance. They admitted that he was a compulsive gambler, but no one knew where or how frequently he gambled. As for possible debts or business worries they could only shrug their shoulders. If Mr. Shing had problems then he had not mentioned them to his employees.

The picture that eventually emerged was that of an ordinary Chinese businessman with one ordinary Chinese vice. It was helped along gently by seemingly vague suggestions and prompting from the charming May Ling, and during its construction we succeeded in making a complete tour of the premises. I saw the cramped factory where sweating Chinese of both sexes worked in grey overalls and long rubber gloves over the hot plastic moulding machine, and then the packaging shed where the end products were sorted and packed into cardboard boxes for export. In the process of ensuring that we missed no one who could possibly have information to offer we looked behind every door and into every corner. I even had the opportunity to glance into the open broom cupboard. I saw everything, but what I did not see was a single trace of either opium or heroin. It was obvious, as no doubt it was intended to be, that the Happy Valley Fruit Company manufactured plastic products only. There was no equipment here for refining heroin, and nowhere to hide it.

To complete my investigation I was allowed to search through Mr. Shing's personal office, his desk, and all his papers. May Ling and the chief clerk looked on hopefully.

"Nothing," I said at last. I closed the lid of the desk and tried to look like a frustrated private detective who had expected to find something. "There's nothing at all that can tell us what has happened to Mr. Shing."

The chief clerk looked disturbed, and May Ling bit nervously at her pretty lip.

"Perhaps there will be something at his apartment," she suggested.

I frowned at the chief clerk, feigning reluctance to admit defeat. "Have there been any unusual visitors lately?" I demanded. "Have you noticed anything unusual at all?"

"No, sir." The chief clerk looked unhappy and spread his hands. "Everything has been normal."

I sighed wearily and then nodded to May Ling.

"Okay, we'll try the apartment."

It took us another hour to return to Hong Kong, where I was careful to allow May Ling to direct me to Paradise Building. We took the elevator to the tenth floor, and walked along the short corridor to room two-three-nine. There, somewhat self-conscious and with downcast eyes, May Ling produced a small silver key to open the door. We went inside.

The apartment consisted of three rooms, a small kitchen and dining area, a large, comfortable bedroom, and a bathroom. It fell short of being luxurious, but there was nothing lacking. We searched it together, as thoroughly as we had examined the Happy Valley Fruit Company, and with the same end result. There were no clues to Mr. Shing's supposed gambling activities, and neither was there anything that could link him to narcotics. After we had opened all the drawers and cupboards, shaken out all the books, and looked under the bed pillows, inside all the ornaments, and under all the carpets, May Ling finally accepted that we were beaten.

"I cannot understand it," she said helplessly. "I thought, that we must find something — a diary or a notebook, some figures or an IOU." She looked lost and afraid. "David, what can we do now?"

"We must think again," I said calmly. "Perhaps the best thing to do is to mix a couple of drinks, relax, and talk the whole matter over."

"Perhaps you are right." She did not sound very sure of herself and looked dubiously around the room. "But not here, David. I would not feel comfortable. Let us leave and go to my apartment."

I nodded agreeably. Tonight I was in a compliant mood.

★ ★ ★

We re-crossed the Straits to Kowloon-side. It was evening and the galaxies of lights reflecting in the black silk waters of the harbour were showing up at their romantic best. We stood very close, shoulder to shoulder, by the rail of the ferry, and then sat

149

even closer in the back of the taxi I hailed on the far side. May Ling told the driver to take us to Empress Building. I was not surprised, for I knew from Sunny that this was the address at which Mr. Shing had spent his last night alive. We were there in five minutes.

The apartment was similar to the one which we had just left, except that it was more feminine with deeper carpets and softer colours. There were vases of tastefully arranged flowers, and overall a pleasing perfume of sandalwood and roses. Propped up against the pillows in the bedroom, and contributing to the little girl lost image, there was a large, cuddly teddy bear.

May Ling produced a bottle of Chinese rice wine, apologizing because she had no stock of strong spirits. I smiled her apologies away and opened the wine. She poured two glasses and we made ourselves comfortable. She looked at me hopefully.

"What are you thinking, David?

What do you think has happened to Mr. Shing?"

"So far there is no evidence that anything has happened to him. I feel that he may yet reappear, safe and well!"

"I wish that I could think so, but his disappearance is so strange that my instinct tells me that something is wrong. I am afraid that he may be dead, or in hiding in fear of his life."

"Because of his gambling debts?"

She nodded.

"But we have found no proof that he does owe money."

She looked bewildered. "But what other possible explanation could there be?"

"That is what we must find out." I paused delicately. "Perhaps you can tell me some more about yourself, and about your personal relationship with Mr. Shing?"

Confusion reflected in her face. "Do you think this is important?"

I nodded. "You are a very beautiful woman, May Ling, and men can become very jealous with beautiful women. I have to consider every possibility."

"But I have no other — admirers."

"Even so, you must have relatives. Does your family approve of your friendship with Mr. Shing?"

"I have no family." She looked down at her wine glass for a moment, and then into my eyes. "I will tell you frankly, David. I came from mainland China seven years ago. I had to leave my family behind. I came alone to Hong Kong, with nothing but my beauty and my wits. I succeeded in making a good marriage. My husband was moderately wealthy, but he took sick and died. He was a business man very similar to Mr. Shing. The money that he left to me enabled me to rent and furnish this apartment, but I knew that although it gave me some independence it would not last for ever."

She hesitated, embarrassed but not ashamed. "Now I am what you would call a — courtesan. I accept gentlemen friends, because until I can find a man that I can truly love, I do not wish to marry again. Since my husband died I have had three such gentleman friends. The first two are now married to other women, so those relationships are closed. Mr. Shing is now my gentleman friend, he brings me presents and gifts of money."

She paused. "Perhaps you do not approve, David, but I am a woman alone in Hong Kong and I have to live. And despite the money and the presents Mr. Shing is a true friend and I am concerned for him."

"I do not disapprove," I said. "And I will help you as much as I can."

She smiled and her hand touched mine. We were sitting side by side on her cushioned divan, and for a moment she leaned her dark head upon my shoulder. Her thigh and knee brushed mine.

"You are very kind, David Chan." she said in a low voice. "I am very glad that I came to you."

I set down my wine glass and gently smoothed her glossy black hair. It seemed that comfort was more appropriate than words. After a moment she lifted up her face again.

"You are also very handsome, David. There is something about a Eurasian man. You have the culture and the grace of the Chinese, yet in your face there is also the strength and character of the English. You are the best of both races."

There was only one way to answer a compliment as direct as that. Also her sweet red lips were too close for me to miss the point and I kissed them slowly but firmly. Her arms slipped around my neck and held tight for a moment, and I could feel her heart beating steadily inside her breast as though she was truly afraid.

"You said that you found me beautiful," she whispered at last. "If you wish to sleep with me you will find me willing."

It was not an unexpected offer and I was still in my compliant mood. I kissed her again.

"I should very much like to sleep with you," I said.

I was philosophically resigned to my fate.

9

IT was a glorious morning, with the massed skyscrapers of Hong Kong and Kowloon glittering white between the bright blue shades of sea and sky. It was the kind of morning when I would normally be up early to savour every fresh minute, but on this particular morning I arrived at the office half an hour late. Belinda and Tracey were already there, pretending to be busy with the filing cabinets and the morning mail. We exchanged the usual greetings and I sat down at my desk to read the few letters, mostly bills, that Belinda had pushed forward for my attention. The girls continued to look busy, but after two minutes their nonchalance collapsed. They exchanged glances and then approached my desk to gaze down at me sternly.

"Well, David?" They said together.

"Well what?" I asked innocently.

"The beautiful Chinese lady?" Belinda said bluntly.

"Miss May Ling," Tracey qualified, just to be sure that I understood.

"Who was she?" Belinda added. "And what did she want?"

I laid down the electricity bill and looked up. "She was a client," I said. "And she wanted to engage our services. Why didn't you stop and listen at the time?"

"Because we're two tactful girls," Tracey answered. "That look she gave us told us quite plainly that she wasn't interested in engaging *our* services — she was only interested in engaging *your* services."

"And we were confident that you could cope."

"Well thank you," I said. I smiled blandly but then the double glint behind Belinda's elegant spectacles warned me that she was becoming impatient. I decided that it was time to explain.

"Miss May Ling wants us to locate a friend of hers who is missing," I told them. "To be more precise he is her gentleman lover who has mysteriously disappeared. His name is Mr. Shing."

They were silent for a full minute while they digested the implications, and then Belinda said slowly:

"Did you take the job?"

I nodded. "Miss May Ling is now paying us one hundred HK dollars per day to search for Mr. Shing."

"But we started off by charging Ralph Slater one hundred *US* dollars," Tracey protested.

I shrugged. "If I asked Miss Ling for one hundred US she wouldn't be able to afford it. And if I asked Ralph Slater for one hundred HK he'd think that we were a cheap agency not worth employing. One price for the locals, and another for the yanks — that's business practice all over the East!"

Tracey frowned, but Belinda refused to concern herself with the dubious injustice of overcharging the wealthy.

"When we came back to the office yesterday afternoon you were out," she said pointedly. "How did you spend the rest of the day?"

"I searched for Mr. Shing," I said. "May Ling accompanied me, and gave me access to all the places where we might have hoped to find a lead. We went to the Happy Valley Fruit Company and talked to everyone there. Then we went to Paradise Building and searched Mr. Shing's apartment. Then we came back to May Ling's own apartment in Empress Building where we know Mr. Shing spent his last night alive. It was a busy day. I had complete freedom to inspect every address we know that has any associations with Mr. Shing."

"And what did you find?"

"Nothing," I admitted calmly. "That was the whole purpose of the exercise. They wanted to show me that there was nothing to find. Somebody made one-hundred-per-cent sure that all those places were clean for my inspection.

They wanted to satisfy me with the conviction that Mr. Shing is truly a dead end."

Belinda had found herself a chair, while Tracey rested one hip on my desk. They were both thoughtful.

"Does May Ling know that Mr. Shing is dead?" Tracey asked.

"I believe so. Either she is involved or she is being used, and I am afraid that she is playing her part so well that I cannot accept that she is merely being used."

Belinda frowned. "Is she aware that we know that Mr. Shing is dead?"

I frowned too, for I had yet to reach any satisfying conclusion on that particular point.

"If they knew that we can connect Mr. Shing with the *Fragrant Lotus* and Cheng-Weng junks, then all this business of proving to me that Mr. Shing is a dead end would be a waste of time," I said slowly. "So, I think that maybe they don't know that I was aboard the junk."

"But three of the crew escaped," Tracey objected. "Surely they must have talked!"

"Not necessarily. Remember that they made some bad mistakes. They had me cornered and failed to kill me. Instead they allowed me to escape. They abandoned their skipper to die, and left their junk to burn out and sink. I rather suspect that the people who employed them can be quite merciless with employees who make blunders like that. It's most likely that the junk crew concocted a better explanation for the fire. An explanation less shameful for them, and one that did not mention my presence at all."

"That's all sheer conjecture," Belinda objected in turn.

"True, but it would explain why May Ling and the people behind her are confident that they can buy us off, simply by demonstrating that all our other leads will lead us nowhere."

There was another silence for contemplation.

"Are you sure about the Happy Valley Fruit Company?" Tracey queried. "That place seemed such a natural cover for smuggling narcotics."

"It wasn't a dual purpose factory that also produced heroin," I said positively. "It didn't have the right facilities. At the same time I suspect that it was a distribution point, and that heroin was smuggled out inside the plastic fruits. The point is that now it's blown, and they won't be using it for that purpose any more. They gave it a final clean-up before I was invited in to take a look."

"Let's get back to Miss May Ling," Belinda said. "Are we still retained by her, and what does she expect us to do now?"

"We are still retained by her, and she expects us to continue searching for her friend Mr. Shing," I said calmly. "We are asked to believe that he was a compulsive gambler, and that his disappearance is in some way related to his presumed gambling debts. I have

162

assured her that we will do all that we can to investigate these possibilities."

"So in effect she is trying to buy up the time that we would otherwise spend in working for Ralph Slater," Belinda estimated correctly.

"But Slater is paying us a much bigger retainer!" Tracey said.

"May Ling doesn't know that," I told her. "She asked me to set my fee, and I quoted what would be our normal price to a local client. Naturally she wants me to concentrate on her problems to the exclusion of any other jobs we may have on hand, and so she is making it worth my while in other ways." I paused delicately. "Mr. Slater may have the most dollars, but in some spheres he cannot hope to compete."

They gave me a double dose of reproving looks.

"David," Belinda said severely. "You haven't allowed yourself to be seduced?"

"I tried to resist," I said bravely. "But I am a mere man after all."

They decided that half a minute of

reproachful silence was in order, and then Tracey continued to speak to me again.

"Does this mean that we study Miss Ling, and abandon Ralph Slater?"

"Not quite." It was my turn to look hurt. "It only means that we endeavour to make that impression to May Ling. We can afford to waste some of our time while we wait."

"For what are we waiting?" Belinda demanded promptly.

"We wait for another telephone call from Sunny Cheong," I informed them. "I put him on the payroll again before I came to the office this morning, He's going to have one of his boys do some casual prowling around Castle Peak Bay — and then he'll let me know when the next Cheng-Weng junk is due to sail."

"And what then?" Tracey said slowly.

"Then I have to find some means of following that junk on its voyage. At the moment we have to establish three points before we can hope to clear up any of the mysteries surrounding this case. One, we have to be sure that the Cheng-Weng junks are regularly shipping opium. Two, we have to find out how and where the junks are unloaded so that they can return to their home port with innocent cargoes of fish. And three, we want to know the location of the factory where the opium is refined into heroin. I don't think we have any hope of establishing any of those points from this end. Mr. Shing is dead, the Happy Valley Fruit Company has been scrubbed down and whitewashed, and May Ling is busily hanging up whole curtains of red herrings. The only course open to us at the moment is to follow a Cheng-Weng junk on a complete round trip."

"That does make sense," Belinda agreed, "but it will also make a very risky operation."

I nodded. "That's why you girls will stay behind and run the office."

They stared at me doubtfully, but

this time they knew better than to argue.

★ ★ ★

We spent the rest of the morning in compiling a list of all the known gambling houses in Hong Kong and Kowloon. It was a necessary precaution, for that afternoon May Ling paid another visit to the office. Again it was Tracey who let her in, and she appeared as demure and beautiful as before. Today her *cheongsam* was primrose yellow, but it fitted her equally well. She smiled at both Tracey and Belinda, and my two partners had the tact and charm to smile just as gracefully in return.

May Ling approached my desk.

"Hello, David. I hope that I am not worrying you too soon?"

"You could never worry me too soon, or too often." I smiled as I rose to greet her, and allowed the smile to imply all that was assumed to be between us alone. I took her hand and squeezed it gently.

Belinda brought her a chair, which she acknowledged gratefully as she sat down.

"David tells us that we are helping you to find a missing friend," Tracey said helpfully.

"Yes," May Ling said. "My friend Mr. Shing has disappeared."

Tracey and Belinda looked sympathetic, and I noticed that this time they were not exhibiting any undue haste to dash off and leave me to cope unaided.

"We have started to make a list of the possible gambling places that Mr. Shing may have frequented," I said in a more business-like tone. I offered the list for her inspection. "When these places are open for business this evening I will try to visit as many of them as I can. I will try to ascertain whether or not Mr. Shing is known to any of them."

May Ling read the list and looked

impressed. "These are good places to start. But I did not come to check on your progress, David. I came because I have remembered something that might be helpful. I did not remember it until after you had gone" — she blushed — "until after you had gone last night."

"What did you remember?" I asked, smoothing over her moment of confusion. "Was it the name of one of Mr. Shing's gambling friends? Or the address of one of the private parties that he attended?"

She shook her head. "No, David, I told you that he did not reveal such details. But I remember that a few weeks ago he went to Macau. He stayed there for several days, and I am sure that his only purpose was to gamble in the big casinos. When he came back he was depressed, which makes me feel that he must have lost much money." She hesitated. "Now that I have remembered this I am sure you must start to look for him in Macau. You must look in the big gambling casinos."

I regarded her thoughtfully for a moment. "If I go to Macau I shall have to take one of my assistants with me," I said at last. "We may have to stay several days in order to make a complete investigation. I would have to charge you for our expenses on top of our retaining fee."

She looked hesitant, but only for a moment.

"I will accept your expenses, David. Mr. Shing is important to me, and I am not afraid to pay to help him."

"Very well then," I smiled at her as though she was my only consideration. "Tonight I will tour these places on my list, and if I learn nothing then tomorrow I will go to Macau."

Tracey and Belinda raised their eyebrows doubtfully, but May Ling was watching my face and her reaction was a grateful smile.

★ ★ ★

Later that afternoon I had a telephone call from Sunny. I listened to him closely for a few moments, then thanked him and asked him to continue keeping watch. May Ling had left the office, but Belinda and Tracey were gazing at me expectantly as I replaced the receiver.

"Events are moving," I told them. "There's a Cheng-Weng junk named the *Yellow Lotus* due to sail from Castle Peak Bay tomorrow night. One of Sunny's friends has just watched the water and provisions being loaded aboard for a five day fishing trip."

"But tomorrow you'll be chasing wild geese in Macau," Belinda reminded me. "Isn't that inconvenient?"

"Not at all," I said blandly. And I told them why it would not be inconvenient, and why I was not even surprised.

10

SHORTLY before eight o'clock the following morning I boarded the sleek, one-hundred-and-twenty-foot long hydrofoil bound for Macau. Tracey Ryan accompanied me, and May Ling came down to the wharf to wave us goodbye. May Ling wore her wine-red *cheongsam* again, and there was moist sincerity in her eyes as she regretted that she would not be joining us on the trip. She preferred to remain in Hong Kong just in case Mr. Shing should reappear, and promised to telephone us immediately at the hotel address I had given her if this should happen. I told her not to worry and kissed her tenderly on the cheek before we parted.

"A scheming little bitch, isn't she?" Tracey said pleasantly when I joined her in the hydrofoil's forward passenger cabin.

"Didn't you know," I said, "that we Chinese are all fiendishly cunning?"

She nodded. "I have heard the rumours."

"We're also impartial," I added, and I kissed her cheek in turn to prove it.

A few moments later the hydrofoil's engines began to throb with life. The craft moved out from the wharf, her sharp bows rising on the stilt-like floats as the stern sank deeper into the water. Poised like a giant speedboat she began to surge forward with the blue waters of the harbour, the junks and the scattered shipping, flashing past on either side. Through the cabin window I caught a final glimpse of May Ling vigorously waving a red chiffon scarf from the wharf.

The forty mile journey across the great, glittering blue estuary of the Pearl River to the tiny Portuguese Colony of Macau, lasted for only seventy-five minutes. The hydrofoil skimmed the waves at thirty-eight knots like some high-spirited mechanical flying fish.

It was nine-fifteen when we arrived, and after passing through the brief formalities of customs and immigration my first task was to book my return passage on an identical craft departing for Hong Kong at ten-forty-five.

I then had ninety minutes in which to call a taxi and escort Tracey to the Chinese Palace hotel. It was one of the smaller hotels, used regularly by the flocks of Chinese visitors who came to Macau to make use of the famed gambling casinos. I had stayed there on previous visits and the manager remembered me. He approached with a wide smile and the outstretched hand of welcome as we entered the small foyer.

"Mr. Chan, it is so nice to see you again."

"Mr. Soong," I accepted his hand. "Please allow me to introduce my secretary, Miss Tracey Ryan."

Mr. Soong smiled wider and bubbled out another welcome. Then he turned to me. "After your radiotelephone call last night we have reserved for you two single rooms, Mr. Chan. They are two of the best rooms in the hotel."

I smiled at him. "I thank you, but there has been a slight change in my plans. Another case has come up in Hong Kong, which means that I must return immediately. Miss Ryan will be staying here alone for a few days."

Mr. Soong looked dismayed, and then embarrassed.

"I am sorry. I had looked forward to having you as my guest again." He paused delicately. "There will have to be a cancellation charge for the second room."

I smiled and drew him quietly to one side. "I understand. In fact I would prefer to pay for both rooms for the five days that Miss Ryan will be staying here. If you can prepare the bill accordingly, in my name, at the end of Miss Ryan's stay — then it will be paid without question."

Mr. Soong gazed at me shrewdly. "My hotel register must be correct,

Mr. Chan. The police will check."

I nodded in agreement. "Of course, I would not ask you to falsify the hotel register. All that I ask is for the double bill made out in my name, for which you will be paid in full." I paused discreetly. "It is a small matter of expenses and public relations. I have two clients who each expect me to be making enquiries in two different places. I do not wish to appear to be neglecting either one."

Mr. Soong understood. "If it is only the bill, then there is no harm if I allow another guest to use the room?"

"None at all," I assured him.

Mr. Soong thought about it and smiled. He didn't see how he could lose by simply selling me a false bill of charge, and if he could at the same time let the room that I had cancelled to another guest then he would make double profit. If this was what I wanted then Mr. Soong was happy, as I had known he would be. He nodded and smiled again, and offered me his hand to indicate that we had an agreement.

I accompanied Tracey up to her room, and after Mr. Soong had left we held a brief conference.

"You know what to do?" I asked her.

Tracey nodded, and opened her handbag to take out a slim pad which she used for jotting down notes.

"According to May Ling, her Mr. Shing came to Macau four weeks ago on the seventh and stayed until the twelfth. I'm to check out this list of possible hotels that you have given me, and find out where he stayed — if he stayed here at all. I'm also to check out all the local casinos, and find out where he gambled, and how much money he gambled — if he gambled at all." She looked up at me wryly. "I'm to spin this job out for five days and then return to Hong Kong. I'm to make sure that I bring back the hotel bill to put in with our expense account — a bill that will seem to prove that you and I spent our time in Macau together."

"That's perfect," I said, and I kissed her. "The only other point is to make sure that you stay out of trouble. I don't think that there is anything here for you to find, but if you do stumble into anything pull back and play safe. If you sense that there's any risk at all I want you to radiotelephone the office where Belinda will be standing by, and then wait until I get back to sort it out."

"Don't worry, David. I can take care of myself." She smiled, and then kissed me, but her lovely green eyes were troubled. "You just make sure that you take care, David. You're the one who is sticking his neck out."

★ ★ ★

After a fast return trip on the speeding hydrofoil I stepped down on to Hong Kong wharf at eleven-thirty. At twelve noon, only four hours after I had departed on my supposed five-day trip to Macau I was back in my office. Belinda was waiting for me with Ralph Slater and Sunny Cheong. Sunny was sitting behind my desk, trying my chair for size. While Slater stood at the window staring down at the harbour. Slater turned round sharply as I entered.

"Hello, David. Belinda has been putting me in the picture, so I know what you're planning."

"That's good." I approved because I had told Belinda to call him. "That saves me all the trouble of explaining." I looked to Sunny. "Did you find me a junk skipper who is prepared to play along?"

Sunny nodded complacently. "There is a large sea-going fishing junk named the *Sea Pearl* standing ready in the typhoon shelter on Kowloon-side. The Captain is a man called Feng Li-Shu. He is also the owner, and answerable only to himself, so there are no complications there. Captain Feng is willing to place his junk and his crew at our disposal for the sum of two-hundred US dollars for each day."

I turned to Slater. "That sounds fair enough to me, considering the risks that may be involved. How about you, Ralph? We'll be spending on your expense account — are you prepared to put up that extra money?"

"Sure I am," Slater could not have sounded more positive. "If this trip is going to fill in those missing blanks then I'd willingly pay double. There's just one thing, David, I want to come along."

"I've tried to convince him that it just isn't a good idea," Belinda said apologetically. "But he doesn't want to believe me."

"Look, if I'm paying for this little sea-cruise then I've got a right. I'm dealing myself in!"

I shook my head gently. "I'm sorry Ralph, but it's not a question of rights. It's a matter of common-sense. There's a strong possibility that this could prove to be more than just a pleasant little sea-cruise."

"That's just my point, and two guns are better than one. You may have got the better of me once, David, but that doesn't mean that I'm not a useful guy to have around."

"I don't doubt that," I said quietly. "In any other circumstances where the going was likely to get rough I'd be glad to have you around. But not on this trip, Ralph. I'm almost certain that at some stage of her round voyage the *Yellow Lotus* is going to lead us into Chinese territorial waters, and there the big danger is that we might be stopped by a Chinese patrol boat. If that happens I can pick up a net, slump my shoulders a bit, and hope to get away as one of the junk's crew. We would just be an innocent fishing junk that has wandered off course."

I paused there and shook my head again, smiling sadly. "With you aboard, Ralph, we'd have no hope at all. You are so obviously American that we'd be blown the moment anyone hostile took a straight look at your face. To then pull out two automatics would be just suicide. In fact, I won't be taking a gun at all. Ordinary crewmen on a fishing junk don't walk around with heavy artillery slung in a shoulder harness, so neither will I."

"Okay," Slater said. "I'll accept that my presence on board the *Sea Pearl* will be an additional risk. But it's one that I'm prepared to take. I still want to come along!"

"Then the deal is off," I said bluntly, "because that additional risk is an unnecessary risk that *I* am *not* prepared to take. I have no intention of spending the next fifty years sitting in some lousy communist jail on the mainland. I also doubt whether Captain Feng will want to accept that risk, plus the risk of losing his junk. I'll give it to you straight, Ralph, you have two options only — either I go alone, or the whole thing ends right here."

Slater glared at me, his hard grey eyes were savage, and his hands were balled unconsciously into fists at his sides. He was angry but he wasn't stupid, and slowly the stiffness eased out of him. He turned to Belinda.

"You warned me that I shouldn't underestimate this guy. I should have listened." He forced her a smile, and made an effort to keep it there as he looked back to me. "You're right, David. I could screw things up just by being there. It sticks in my gut to stay behind, but I guess that's the way it's got to be." He paused. "Just remember that Marion was my daughter. They killed her with their Goddamned heroin, and I'm still trying to get even. For me it's personal!"

"I won't forget that," I promised. "I'll let you know what happens as soon as I get back."

He accepted that reluctantly, and then made an effort to be practical. "How do you intend to follow the Cheng-Weng junk? If you keep her in sight for five days then surely her crew will get suspicious. You could also lose her at night."

I circled my desk and Sunny shifted himself to make room. Sitting down I pulled open a lower drawer and lifted out a small black box fitted with a red bulb and dials.

"Here's your answer," I told Slater calmly. "This is the radio receiver to a homing device. The transmitter is a simple bug which will be hidden aboard the *Yellow Lotus*. It emits a slow bleep signal at five-second intervals, and the receiver can pick it up from a ten mile radius. The receiver of course will be with me aboard the *Sea Pearl*. With this we can trail the *Yellow Lotus* by day or by night without ever coming within sighting distance."

"The transmitter should already be in position," Sunny added casually. "A friend of mine took it out to Castle Peak Bay this morning, while I was seeking out Captain Feng in the typhoon shelter."

"You guys are well-equipped, and well-organized," Slater said. He seemed satisfied, even though he had lost an argument. "I guess you have to be getting aboard that junk pretty soon, David. Is there anything I can do until you get back?"

"I don't think so. Until I get back with some more information there's nothing that any of us can do. When I do get back I'll be in touch."

"Okay," he looked hesitant for a moment. "I'll wish you luck."

★ ★ ★

After Slater had gone I turned my attention to Belinda. She had been waiting patiently behind her desk with her chin held in her cupped hands. Her eyes regarded me gravely through her golden butterfly spectacles.

"You know what you have to do?" I asked her.

She nodded. "While you're away I answer the mail and answer the telephone. I also keep a discreet watch on Ralph Slater." She paused. "I could also keep a discreet watch on your delightful Miss May Ling?"

"No," I said flatly. "That could be dangerous. I don't want any moves made in that direction until I get back. While I'm away from Hong Kong you will take no risks — is that understood?"

"Yes, David," she said so meekly that I couldn't believe her.

"I mean it Belinda," I said seriously. "Stay out of trouble. And if trouble does blow up without you looking for it, don't hesitate to call for Sunny. He may look fat and slow, but he isn't, and he can have half a dozen fast young Chinese from the gymnasium on your doorstep in a matter of minutes."

"I will look after her," Sunny promised.

Belinda realized that we were not joking, and some of the laughter went out of her eyes.

"Alright, David," she said soberly.

"I'll be careful. But please — take care of yourself."

★ ★ ★

An hour later I was on board the *Sea Pearl*, a fifty-foot fishing junk, seaworthy and kept in good order. Her nets were tidy and her decks were clean. The large squared mainsail of brown canvas, stiffened by bamboo rods, was already hoisted. The junk was only waiting for my arrival. Sunny came on board just long enough to introduce me to the Captain and three-man crew, and as soon as he had returned to the quayside the auxiliary engine was started and the junk set sail.

Once we had cleared the junk and sampan cluttered waters of the typhoon shelter the *Sea Pearl* turned north west, heading through the green offshore islands towards Castle Peak Bay. It would not have been wise to hire out another junk from Castle Peak, where all the junk skippers would almost certainly be known to each other, and so we now had a twenty mile cruise around the shoreline of the New Territories before we would be in a position to intercept the *Yellow Lotus* when she sailed. It was a beautiful afternoon, and with four hours to sunset and the gentle chug of the engine assisting the spread sail there was plenty of time. I stripped to my shorts and lay out on the open deck to soak up the hot sun.

I awoke with Captain Feng pulling politely at my arm. The air had turned cool and the sun was setting in a glorious blaze of red and pink fire behind the darkening waves to the west.

I realized that the engine had stopped and that the *Sea Pearl* was riding at anchor. I looked along the shoreline and saw the open mouth of the bay, where the slanted masts of the packed junks were caught in silhouette against the sunset like the slender black trunks of a forest on fire.

"Castle Peak," Feng said politely, and indeed the stark, black hump of the peak itself was unmistakable.

I smiled my thanks, and then brought out the homing signal receiver. I turned a dial on the black box and immediately the steady *bleep-bleep-bleep* came through firm and clear. Somewhere in the black tangle of the shipping the hidden transmitter bug was sending out its signal, and just in case I was deaf the red bulb on top of the receiver also began to flash faintly and intermittently. Captain Feng and his crew clustered around curiously and I explained how it worked.

"Very clever," Feng said admiringly.

"Made in Japan," I said, and they all smiled.

★ ★ ★

We waited as the sunset faded into darkness. Night settled over the silent

188

sea, and gradually the stars came out. I watched the mouth of the bay and the occasional shadow of an emerging junk or sampan. An hour passed, another, and then the hands of my wristwatch began to tick away the minutes of the third. Then abruptly the bleeping from the homing receiver began to strengthen, and the red warning light began to blink more rapidly. I saw the distant, ghostly shape of another junk moving slowly out from the harbour and the black shelter of the peak, and knew that that junk could only be the *Yellow Lotus*.

I nodded to Captain Feng, and immediately he ordered his men to turn the sail to catch the wind.

11

THE *Yellow Lotus* vanished into the darkness, but all through that night the *Sea Pearl* trailed her on a due westerly course by means of the homing signal. The wind was favourable and the sea was moderately calm, and the two junks made a steady five knots without any help from the auxiliary engines. We were crossing the wide mouth of the Pearl River once more, and frequently saw the twinkles of light that marked other fishing vessels. When dawn came it was a filtering of grey light that gradually turned the dark waves to brightening blue. I turned my head to look back over the high stern, and saw that there the sea and the sky were again awash with running rivers of fire. Out here sunrise was as spectacular as sunset.

Captain Feng Li-Shu was at the

wheel. He was a stocky man of about forty-five with a brown, weathered face and bristly hair. I had already learned that his family had originally come from Canton, and that he had been sailing junks since he was ten years old. The *Sea Pearl* was his pride and joy, taking preference over the wife and three children he had ashore. He pointed a brown finger out over the starboard bow.

"Macau is over there, about ten miles away."

I glanced idly at my wristwatch. It had taken us approximately eight hours to cruise the distance the hydrofoil had streaked in seventy five minutes. However, I had by now attuned myself to the long swell of the waves and the slow, lazy movements of the junk. I had no complaints.

Feng pointed again, far ahead to where the square shape of a diminutive sail could just be seen.

"There," he said. "That is the junk with the bleep."

I produced the powerful binoculars I had brought along for moments like this, and brought the distant junk into focus. She was about six miles away on the horizon, and the polished optics pulled her to within half a mile, which was still not quite close enough to distinguish the individual figures on her decks. In size and shape she was the identical twin of her ill-fated sister ship, the *Fragrant Lotus*, whose burned-out hulk now lay on the sea bed below Castle Peak.

"She does not stop at Macau." Feng pointed out the obvious simply to make conversation.

"No," I said. "My guess is that she will lead us along the South China coast."

"But why? She has already passed good fishing grounds."

"She is not on a fishing trip."

"Ah, I see." Feng nodded his head knowingly, and then looked at me again. "Opium?"

I nodded, because Feng was no fool,

and it was the obvious second choice cargo. In fact I would not have been surprised if Captain Feng had not run a few smuggling trips of his own during his thirty-five years at sea.

"Opium is not bad," Feng said conversationally. "I know many men who like to smoke a pipe of opium."

"Opium in itself is not so bad," I agreed tactfully. "But opium that is then refined into heroin is very bad indeed. You would not wish for your wife or your sons to take heroin!"

Feng frowned at the thought, and then nodded bleakly. However, I doubted whether he was very concerned with the morals of the business. He was being paid two-hundred dollars per day to do my bidding, which was more than he could hope to make catching fish, and the crew of the *Yellow Lotus* were strangers from a different port. Captain Feng was quite happy to prove himself compliant.

He looked thoughtfully at the binoculars in my hand.

"Perhaps some man on the other junk will also have a pair of these?"

"That's a good point," I conceded. "Hold back and let the other junk get over the horizon."

Feng nodded and called orders to his crew. The sail was lowered and the *Sea Pearl* began to rock erratically as she drifted at the mercy of the long waves. We watched and waited as the sail on the horizon gradually vanished. The bleep signal and the red light bulb on top of my homing receiver which lay on a shelf in the wheelhouse, gradually became fainter. Not until our quarry was almost out of range did I give Feng the word. Then the sail was hoisted and we continued the pursuit.

It was another warm, sunny day, and I took advantage of it to strip down for some more sleep and sun-bathing while the slow chase ran ever westward over the South China Sea.

★ ★ ★

At noon one of the crewmen prepared a meal of rice and fish, and glasses of hot tea. The sun was scorching the sky and so we ate in the forward cabin, sitting cross-legged on the floor with our chopsticks and rice bowls. We were still eating when there was a sudden shout of alarm from the man we had left at the wheel. I won the fast scramble to the open deck, beating the Captain by a short head, and saw the sharp grey bows of a Chinese patrol boat sweeping up fast on our starboard side.

I spun on my heel while the others gaped and dived into the wheelhouse. The helmsman was still holding to his course, and his eyes flashed with sudden resentment and fear as he tore his gaze away from the gunboat to look at me. I ignored him and deftly scooped up the binoculars and the even more incriminating homing receiver that still lay on the narrow shelf by his elbow. I flicked off the dials and the bleep became silent. The receiver box and the binoculars I dropped into a nearby bucket that I had positioned earlier for this type of emergency. I picked up the bucket and walked back on deck, carrying the bucket carelessly as though it contained nothing more sinister than galley slops and refuse. The gunboat had overshot the mark and was losing speed as she circled back to come up on our port bow. I paused on our starboard side, ready to tip the contents of the bucket into the sea.

"Captain Feng," I said softly. "Have we entered their territorial waters?"

He shook his head. "No, Mr. Chan, we are still fifteen miles off the coast of mainland China. They have no right — "

He stopped there and shrugged his shoulders, accepting that although the patrol boat had no legal right to interfere with our course, it did have all the necessary power. It was one-hundred foot of fast fighting ship, fitted with four side-launched torpedoes and two forty-mm. anti-aircraft guns. A handful of ratings lined her rail, and from the bridge I saw the white flashes of sunlight reflecting from the powerful glasses held by her officers. I hoped that they had not had those glasses trained on our decks during the split second that I had made my guilty dive into the wheelhouse.

Captain Feng and his crew could only stand helplessly and stare as the gunboat drew level. I lifted my bucket, seated it on the gunwale, and then I grinned stupidly and raised my free hand to wave at the men on the gunboat's bridge. The two officers had lowered their glasses, which were now unnecessary, and simply stared down with blank faces as the two ships passed with an intervening distance of less than twelve feet. I allowed my smile to falter hesitantly and lowered my hand. Some of the ratings lining the gunboat's rail grinned in turn at our obvious discomfort, and then the patrol boat had passed us by and was gathering speed again.

"They were just curious," Feng said at last. "And they wanted to watch us jump. It happens often."

He shrugged his shoulders to pretend that he had not been scared. And I nodded politely to pretend that I believed him. We watched the gunboat diminish in size down the long spearhead of its white wake, and when it vanished I brought my bucket inboard and carried it back to the wheelhouse. I returned the homing receiver to its original resting place and retuned the dials. We were still on course and the slow *bleep-bleep-bleep* began again. The red bulb pulsed dimly.

"Let us finish our rice," I said calmly.

Feng nodded, maintaining his brave front, and he led us back to our interrupted meal.

★ ★ ★

When night came the *Yellow Lotus* was still leading us on the same

198

steady course west-by-south, keeping safely clear of the twelve-mile limit of Chinese territorial waters. Captain Feng was at the wheel and the crew kept themselves amused by squatting in a circle on the open deck to roll dice for rice grains. I slept, anticipating some possible night activity, and was not surprised when I was eventually awoken by some urgent shaking from one of the crew. It was pitch black on deck when I made my way to the wheelhouse.

"I think that the other junk has stopped," Feng informed me on arrival, and he pointed to the receiver that was now bleeping more strongly than before.

"Close the gap," I said quietly. "And have your men stand by to lower the sail."

He nodded and passed on the orders, while I picked up my binoculars and went to the bows. There was a freshening breeze in my face and a cloud bank hid the stars. I waited for half an hour while the junk forged slowly through the soft hiss of the waves, and then tried scanning the dark sea with the glasses. I could see nothing, but when I returned to the wheelhouse to check the red light and the bleep signal were very positive. I knew that the *Yellow Lotus* must be close, and told Feng to lower the sail and let the *Sea Pearl* drift with the waves.

Back in the blunt bows I used the binoculars again, cursing the banked cloud and wishing that there was at least a glimmer of starlight. Behind me the ropes and timbers of the *Sea Pearl* creaked gently as she rode with the swell. Five minutes passed, and then abruptly I saw a flash of yellow light. I focussed the binoculars and realized that at last I had spotted the *Yellow Lotus*. She was hove to with just an oil lamp burning on her masthead. I stared hard, and tasted the sudden bile of exasperation as I saw that her nets were out.

"The junk is fishing," I told Feng, who had handed over the wheel and now stood at my side.

Feng shrugged. "She is a fishing junk!"

"But she didn't come all this way just to fish."

I spoke positively, but I was experiencing doubt. I had been confident that tonight the *Yellow Lotus* would creep in to the Chinese mainland to take on a cargo of opium, but if I was wrong then all my time would be wasted. I raised my glasses and stared at the distant junk again, but no matter how hard I stared she remained hove to, with her decks quiet and innocent, and those damned nets cast out into the sea.

I frowned, but then I decided that there was only one answer. Timing must be important, and the skipper of the Cheng-Weng junk had time to waste before keeping his appointment, which could be later tonight, or even, tomorrow night. To waste that time he was calmly fishing in safe waters. There was nothing to do except pull back and wait for him to resume his voyage. I explained my belief to Feng and he accepted it without argument. He gave soft orders, and using the wind and the sail the *Sea Pearl* began to veer off to a safe distance.

* * *

The night was uneventful, and at dawn our homing signal suddenly began to fade, indicating that the *Yellow Lotus* had hauled up her nets and was continuing on her old course west-by-south. The crew of the *Sea Pearl* ran to hoist our own sail and haul in the sea anchor, and the long, slow chase began again.

The crew kept a wary eye for the return of the Chinese gun-boat, but on this, our second day at sea, we were undisturbed. Having been awake for most of the night I tried to cat-nap through most of the day. Late in the afternoon Feng produced a chessboard and surprised me by playing a very good game of chess. The sun bleached the white decks, and the blue wave-flecked sea was endless.

* * *

Night came, hard on the heels of another blaze of red after the sun sank into the western sea. It was the beginning of our third night, and Feng estimated that we had sailed well over two hundred miles parallel to the China coast. I knew that within the next few hours the turning point must be reached, and so I stayed with Feng in the wheelhouse. The receiving signal bleeped steadily, and the red bulb flashed, and the darkness closed around us like a shroud. After two more hours the signal and the bulb slowly began to fade out.

"The other junk is moving out of range," Feng said. "She cannot gain speed, and so she must have turned aside, either to port or starboard."

"She will turn to shore," I told him. "Change your course to starboard."

He nodded, ordered his men to stand by to change the set of the sail, and then spun the wheel. Once on the new course the homing signal and the warning light again became constant. Some of the tension eased out of me, but not all. Half an hour passed, and I sensed that Feng was growing nervous beside me.

"Mr. Chan," he said at last. "We are inside the twelve-mile limit."

"I know," I said calmly.

He turned to stare at me in the darkness, and I was aware that the rest of the crew were close and listening.

"If the patrol boat catches us here we shall be arrested," Feng said slowly. "I do not want to lose my ship. I do not want to go any further."

"We have not seen the patrol boat today," I reminded him. "The patrol boat is a long way from here. There is no risk, but if you continue to follow the other junk I will pay you an additional five hundred US dollars when we return to Hong Kong."

Feng was silent, he stared out into the night with his lips compressed. "Six hundred," he said at last.

I had expected him to shy at the last minute, and I had expected him to bargain. "Six hundred," I agreed, and offered him my hand.

After that we continued in silence, until suddenly the bleep signal began to strengthen. Feng ordered the sail half lowered and the *Sea Pearl* slowed to a drifting crawl. I went to the bows and used my glasses. Slowly I distinguished the darker line of blackness that was the Chinese mainland.

I returned to Feng. "We are about two miles offshore," I told him quietly. I looked to the homing receiver which was bleeping steadily. "The other junk must have landed. I must follow it all the way."

"No," Feng said. "I will not risk a landing. What excuse will I have if we are caught?" He signed to his men to drop the sail the last few feet, and I saw from the dark set of his face that he was adamant.

I went back to the bows and stared out over the black sea. I felt that it was imperative that I witnessed whatever activity was taking place aboard the *Yellow Lotus*, and if Captain Feng would not take his own junk any further inshore then there was only one other way to get there. I heard a movement and realized that Feng had followed me. He looked embarrassed now, and apologetic, but I knew that he would not change his mind. From his point of view there were limits, and I could not blame him.

"Do you have a large torch?" I asked him.

He nodded, and sent a crewman to fetch it. When the man returned I held the face of the torch low to the deck and tested the bulb and battery. It was a heavy, rubber-handled torch that should prove fairly waterproof, and it was in good working order. I pushed it securely into my waistband, and began to remove my jacket and shoes.

"When I return I will flash the light," I said quietly. "That will be your signal to light the oil lamp to guide me back to the ship. In the meantime cast out your nets and pretend to fish."

Feng understood and looked troubled. "It is a long way to swim, and there may be bad currents — or sharks."

"I must take those risks."

He continued to look unhappy. "Mr. Chan, I must leave here before dawn. I must get the *Sea Pearl* back outside China's twelve mile limit before it is daylight."

"I understand," I said. "I will return in good time."

I patted him on the shoulder to assure him that all would be well, and then I climbed over the side and lowered my body into the sea. I raised my hand once in farewell and smiled at the four anxious faces, and then I released my hold on the gunwale, turned, and thrust myself away from the curved hull. I began to swim strongly for the unseen shore.

12

THE sea was running a long swell, and as much as possible I allowed the waves to carry me in towards the land. An overarm crawl would have been fine for a fast spurt of speed, and the breast stroke would have been best for a slow, silent approach, but I discarded both styles in favour of a firm, rhythmic side-stroke which I found best for conserving my strength. With one shoulder down I could turn my face up to the hidden stars and let my head rest on the surface of the sea. It was a lazy way of swimming, but I was not attempting a sprint record for the shore. It was only important to get there, and to still be fit for any possible action when I arrived.

The *Sea Pearl* was soon lost behind me, swallowed up in the blackness. I was alone with the sea and the night, and after the first few minutes I forgot the suggested dangers of currents and sharks and my body became attuned to the motion of the waves. It was a comforting sensation, like returning to a vast, watery womb. The murmuring sea was my mother, soothing me and ready to embrace and enfold me whenever I needed rest. During the first mile of that long haul to the shore I had no fear of drowning.

After the first hour I began to glance regularly at my wristwatch. I calculated that at my present rate I would cover a mile in forty-five minutes, and so I could only measure distance in time. I tried raising my head and shoulders up from the waves, but I could see nothing except the merging blackness of sea and sky. There was no darker line of land. I was becoming cold, and I began to wish for just one star. The sea was no longer quite so comforting, and I was no longer quite so resigned to its embrace.

When the hands of my wristwatch

passed an hour and thirty minutes I began to worry. By my reckoning I should have covered two miles, and still there was no sign of the shore. If I had misjudged the distance then I was in trouble. I could swim for a few more hours yet, but I remembered that I had to be back on board the *Sea Pearl* well before dawn. I began to lift my head more frequently to search for land.

Quite suddenly I swam into mist, grey swirls of fog vapour blanketing the sea which quickly thickened and blotted out my already limited range of visibility. It was unexpected and gave another jolt to my composure. I paused for a moment, allowing my body to float, but it was too late to turn back now. A wave slapped in my face but I spat out the salt water and swam on.

Five minutes later my feet suddenly struck bottom. For a split second I felt panic as my swimming rhythm was knocked out of joint, and then relief as I realized that my swim was over. I straightened up, standing erect with the waves still breaking around my thighs. I could see now where those waves were breaking white on the mist-shrouded sand, and slowly I walked out on to the beach.

I knelt down on the wet sand and rested, waiting until my breathing returned to normal. While I waited I listened but I could hear nothing. I cursed the mist which would muffle any sounds which might be made, and which was reducing my range of vision to a few yards. It was an eerie sensation to be crouching alone in the swirling silence. I might have landed on another planet, or in another time.

After a few minutes I decided to move. I was feeling the chill and I could not afford to linger. I marked a line in the sand with my heel, for to re-enter the sea at the same point that I had emerged would prove my best hope of returning to the *Sea Pearl*. I had not sensed the pull of any current or tide, and had to trust that I had been swimming in a reasonably straight line. Before I had left the *Sea Pearl* the bleep of the homing signal had indicated that the *Yellow Lotus* was somewhere to the right, and so I turned right now and began to walk swiftly but silently along the sand.

I paced out a thousand yards before I saw the dim glow of diffused yellow light ahead and to my left. I paused and approached with more stealth. As yet nothing took positive shape, but I heard faintly the mutter of voices and the creak of ropes in the fog. The sea was several yards to my right, but suddenly I stepped knee deep into water. I stopped, alarmed by the faint splash I had inadvertently made, but now the muffling mist was in my favour.

I took another cautious step forward, and sank up to my thighs. I realized that there was a deep channel running inland diagonally from the sea, and leading directly towards the light and the low sounds of activity. I backed up on to solid ground again and began to follow the edge of the channel. The sand beach was narrow at this point, and the channel led into a reed-fringed creek which I sensed more than saw lay between two low hills. After a few yards the yellow glow ahead became distinguishable as an oil lamp hanging on a ship's mast. I made out the high, squared stern of a junk almost filling the width of the narrow creek, and I knew that I had found the *Yellow Lotus*.

I crouched down among the tall reeds and edged closer. Now that I had turned between the hills I could see more moving lights which I guessed were the hooded beams of torches. I saw that two plank gangways now spanned the gap between the bank of the creek and the junk's hull, and that there were men struggling to manhandle large sacks on to the junk's deck. More men were roping the sacks together and lowering them into the open hold.

I had no doubt that those sacks must contain the compressed cakes of raw opium, but what suddenly interested me even more were the three men who were supervising the loading operation. Men who were obviously the junk's crew, plus a gang of paid coolies in the traditional wide straw hats were doing the heavy work, but the three silent men who watched over them carried machine pistols slung over one shoulder, and wore the battered remnants of what had once been uniforms. None of the three were young men. Two of them I guessed to be in their fifties, while their leader who stood taller and more aloof was a grizzled old veteran with a wisp of white beard who must have been at least sixty. The old man wore a peaked cap with a polished badge and braid, and on the shoulders of his soiled old battle jacket there were epaulettes with rows of polished stars. I realized with a sense of amazement that I was looking at a fully-fledged General of the old

Kuomintang Army.

It was a strange scene to witness, played out in the ghostly yellow light from the masthead that penetrated for only a few scarce feet before being defeated by the misty darkness. It was conducted in silence except for the gasps and grunts of the toiling coolies, and the occasional ripple of wind-stirred water against the junk's hull. The three men from an army that had been defeated more than twenty years before were relics from the past, and although they wore their ancient caps and jackets proudly, the garments were all creased and stained as though many times they had been hastily bundled up and stuffed into hiding.

I tried to grasp the meaning of what I saw, and recalled the briefing that Tracey had given in my office in order to paint the general picture of the drugs racket. She had mentioned rumours of the trapped Kuomintang forces who had been cut off in southern China after General Chiang Kai-Shek and the bulk of the nationalist armies had retreated to Taiwan at the end of the great civil war that had brought the Communists to power in what was now Red China. The rumours claimed that some of those isolated military groups who had found themselves in Yunnan province on the fringe of the rich poppy-growing hills of the golden triangle had moved in to monopolize the local opium trade with military methods. Now those rumours became reality, for there was no other way in which I could explain the presence of the grim-faced old Kuomintang General who was so obviously in charge of this present operation.

I watched for several minutes, and then decided that it was time to steal away. I could no longer have any possible doubt that the *Yellow Lotus* was in fact smuggling opium, and all that remained now was to follow her back to Hong Kong and note where and how she discharged her cargo. I allowed the reeds and tall bulrushes to close in front of my face and started to ease back into the night, and then I became aware that another figure had moved out of the junk's cabin on to the open deck. The old General half turned, and his hard face softened into a smile of affection. I paused, parted the reeds again, and continued to watch.

The new arrival was muffled in a long dark shawl, and yet the slim figure was faintly familiar. She moved into the pool of light from the masthead and I saw by the outline of her breasts that it was a woman. The old General shifted his machine pistol further back over his right shoulder, and put his left arm around her waist. He spoke softly to her and she smiled. He bent his head and kissed her fondly, and lifting his left hand smoothed the dark shawl away from her black hair. I saw her face briefly as she lifted her lips to his kiss. The woman was May Ling.

I stared at this new twist to the

scene, and my mind started to race with questions. I wanted to remain watching, hoping to overhear something of the conversation, and yet reason told me that they would keep their words to a minimum and in hushed voices. The heavy task of loading was being conducted as silently as possible, and clearly the old General and his friends could not expect the co-operation or approval of the Communist authorities if they were caught. The Red Chinese might adopt an attitude of bland blindness to the actual act of opium smuggling, but the wearing of the old Kuomintang uniforms, even after twenty years, would be classed as reactionary treason.

Reluctantly I closed the curtain of reeds again and began to back away. I had learned as much as I could hope to learn and it was dangerous to linger. My knowledge would be useless if I were to be caught.

I retreated along the bank of the creek as stealthily as I had arrived, until the masthead light was once again a mere yellow glow diffused by the fog. The white vapours were rising more thickly, indicating that the land was very low and marshy. The sounds of activity from the junk became muffled and I turned as I regained the beach. I knew that I had to be back on board the *Sea Pearl* before the *Yellow Lotus* finished loading and returned to sea, and I felt that I was now safe to straighten up and hurry away. As I turned I collided heavily with a silently prowling guard.

He was a young Chinese, too young to own a Kuomintang cap, but he did carry a machine pistol identical to those of the three old soldiers on the junk. Unfortunately for him he was carrying it casually with the muzzle pointed at the soft ground at his feet. Our abrupt meeting was as much of a surprise to him as it was to me. I was not expecting a guard in such an isolated spot, and he no doubt assumed that his patrol was unnecessary boredom.

He gave a startled gasp and tried to bring up the machine pistol. My reaction was faster. I sprang for him and I was three feet in the air when I kicked the fumbling machine pistol from his hands in a classic move of Thai boxing. As I came down again my forward momentum carried him bodily into the creek.

The double splash drowned his attempted cry of alarm, and the sound changed into a choking gurgle as he went under. My weight pushed us both beneath the surface and we squirmed together in a tangled heap in the drowning surge of salt blackness. He broke away from me and we struggled up separately. We were waist-deep in water and my opponent was spluttering and coughing. It would have cost me my own life to let him raise the alarm, and while he was still spitting up the sea from his lungs I hit him across the jaw with all the weight I could muster behind my right fist. He went over and under again and once more I threw myself on top of him. My hands groped for his throat, found a hold, and then fought desperately to hold him down. His thrashing legs broke through the surface and I felt panic and the certainty that his kicking and splashing must be heard. His hands were locked on to my wrists, striving to break my hold, and taking a deep breath I threw my weight down on top of him again and sank us both to the sandy bottom of the creek.

His struggles became more feeble, but I held on for another two minutes until my own starved lungs felt near to bursting. Then I floated up to let my head break free for a moment while I gulped more air. The guard made another squirming spasm of movement that was a matter of instinct more than a conscious effort to get his own head up. I pushed him back to the bottom and held him there for another sixty seconds. By then he was still, and when I released him only the hump of his shoulders rose above the surface.

I stood silent for a few more moments, my heart beating fast and my head pounding as I stared along the mist-blanketed waters of the creek. The yellow light from the junk was all but invisible, and there was no sound to indicate that the brief battle had been heard. I swallowed hard and drew several deep breaths, and then I turned and began to tow the drowned body of the young guard silently out to sea. Fifty yards offshore I released him and allowed him to drift away. Then I swam back to the beach and began to run quickly along the sand, away from the channel and the creek.

It was a painful run that soon degenerated into a wincing limp. I paused to look back over my shoulder, listening to ensure that I was not being followed, and then I continued at a walk. I told myself that in future I would think twice before I kicked anything as hard and as sharp-edged and solid as a machine pistol with my bare feet.

Despite my discomfort I remembered to count out the return pace to a thousand yards. The mist was thick and still rising but I walked slowly to locate the deep line I had ploughed in the sand to mark the point where I had to re-enter the sea. I smoothed the line over and then walked out into the waves. The cold water soothed my bruised toes, and swimming proved a mercifully easier exercise than walking.

13

AFTER another hour and a half swimming I paused wearily to tread water and groped for the torch at my waistband. I had cleared the thick bank of mist clamped over the shoreline after the first half mile, and the higher cloud formations had started to disperse so that now I had a few comforting glimpses of the starlit heavens. Even so the heaving waves were still black and ominous all around me, and there was no sign of the *Sea Pearl*. I was careful not to drop the torch, which was my only lifeline, and then I began to flash the beam in a slow half circle all round.

Five minutes passed, five frustrating minutes filled with the growing fear that Captain Feng and his crew must have panicked and abandoned me to my fate. Then abruptly I saw the answering light. It was to my left instead of to my right where I had expected it to be, and it was still half a mile ahead. I found myself smiling broadly with relief, and then I flicked my torch rapidly on and off several times to let Feng know that I had spotted his signal. Then I tucked the torch back into my waistband and began to swim strongly.

Ten minutes later I was being hauled dripping over the junk's side. Feng had hauled in his nets and sailed to meet me, and he and his crew were also grinning broadly as they fished me out of the waves. Feng confided cheerfully that I was the only catch they had made that night.

I needed a few minutes to catch my breath, and then I told him to put out the oil lamp that was still burning brightly at the masthead. When that was done and the junk was plunged back into darkness I made an effort at answering their combined barrage of questions. I told them how I had located the other junk and watched her hold being loaded with sacks of opium, but I refrained from mentioning the old Kuomintang General, or the young guard I had killed. They had earned the right to demand some satisfaction to their burning curiosity, but there was no cause for me to tell them any more than was necessary.

When all their questions were answered I went into the wheelhouse. There the black box with its bleep signal and the intermittent red light was still functioning at the same intensity.

"The other junk has not moved," said Feng at my shoulder.

"But she will sail before dawn," I assured him. "Her captain will be as anxious as you are to be out of China's twelve-mile limit before daylight."

"We can sail now?" Feng asked hopefully. He looked up at the heavens and added, "Only three hours to dawn."

I nodded. "Head out to sea. We can wait where it is safe."

Feng smiled and gave orders, and suddenly the crew were all happy faces as the dark shadow of the sail was hoisted and the junk got under way.

* * *

We were eight miles off the coast of China when Feng called me into the wheelhouse again. He pointed out that the bleep signal and the red light had stopped fading away and were now constant again. It could only mean that the *Yellow Lotus* had backed out of the creek and was following us out to sea. I explained to Feng and told him to hold his course.

I went back on to the open deck and stared thoughtfully at the hidden mainland. I was still worried about the guard I had killed, for if he had been missed or his body found before the *Yellow Lotus* had sailed, then May Ling and those aboard the Cheng-Weng junk would know that something was wrong, and might well be more alert on the voyage back. It was a fear that I had to keep to myself, for I could gain nothing by alarming Captain Feng and his crew.

I finally decided that the main concern of the old Kuomintang General would be to get the illicit junk back on to the open sea as quickly as possible, and so there was a fair chance that he would not take a roll call of his men until it was too late. By the time he had realized that his guard had been killed the *Yellow Lotus* would be over the horizon, and so he would not be able to inform those on board until she made her next trip. That was the most likely course of events, and I could only hope that my luck was still running good.

I remained on deck until we cleared China's territorial waters, and then told Feng to hold back and manoeuvre the *Sea Pearl* so that the *Yellow Lotus* could move up and resume the lead. By watching the homing receiver we ensured that the two junks did not pass too close, and when the grey light of dawn at last spilled over the sea we were again shadowing our quarry from a safe distance. Our new course was due east into the sunrise.

I yawned, told Feng to keep below the horizon but not to let the signals fade out altogether, and then I turned into the cabin to get some sleep.

The return trip was as smooth and even less eventful than the voyage out. We saw nothing more of the Chinese patrol boat, and the few vessels that we did pass were peaceful fishing junks basking in the sun with their nets over the side. The *Yellow Lotus* kept a steady course ahead and beyond the hazy line of merging sea and sky, without the homing signal we would never have known that she was still there. Even the winds had changed to help us home with a minimum of tacking, and it all seemed so easy that I began to suspect that we must run into a storm. When I was not sleeping or merely being idle I continued to play chess with Captain Feng. The crew rolled more dice and two days passed slowly.

When the sun sank behind us at the end of the second day we had passed Macau on our port side and were again crossing the forty-mile mouth of the great Pearl River. With the onset of darkness I told Feng to close the gap, and the auxiliary engine was started to give us the additional push. The steady *bleep-bleep-bleep* of the homing signal increased in decibels as the distance between the *Sea Pearl* and the *Yellow Lotus* narrowed.

I went forward with my binoculars. It was a reasonably clear night with stars but no moon. I searched the black sea, and after ten minutes I picked out the dark outline of the *Yellow Lotus* cruising ahead under full sail. She was only a mile away, but now that we were approaching Hong Kong I did not dare to let her get out of my physical sight. I called back to Feng to cut off the engine, and returning to sail power only the *Sea Pearl* lost way and maintained her distance.

I remained in the bows, focussing my binoculars every few minutes, and waited.

Two hours passed, and Feng told me that we were well within the territorial waters of Hong Kong. Our course was taking us back to Castle Peak Bay, but as yet there was still plenty of time for the *Yellow Lotus* to divert. I was expecting some kind of diversion, possibly to one of the offshore islands. I felt that now I dared not relax, for if the *Yellow Lotus* gave us the slip over these last few miles, then all of the long journey and the past four days would have gone to waste. Watching the loading of the opium cargo had been necessary only for my own satisfaction, to ensure that I was on the right track, and it was the discharge of that cargo that I had to witness before I could hope to deliver any kind of mortal blow to the big drugs syndicate. There had been plenty of time to think matters over during the slow voyage, and I had resolved to make the destruction of the syndicate my one firm target. The question marks surrounding Ralph Slater and the charming May Ling were now irrelevancies that I merely hoped to clear up on the way.

At the start of this case I had rejected the suggestion that I should aim for the big fish of the syndicate, but now that events had put me on to a hot trail I felt a moral responsibility to follow it through to its conclusion. Regardless of what Slater really wanted, or of May Ling's involvement, I was now out to smash open the organization that thrived on the sale of living death.

I kept a constant watch, and I was still staring straight ahead over the darkened sea when the first brief flashes of light began to dance in the distant blackness. I raised the glasses, searched but could distinguish nothing, and then called softly to Feng.

"Is there an island there?" I asked him.

Feng frowned and shook his head.

I did not ask him how he could be absolutely sure of his present position, but I believed him. So far he had proved himself to be an excellent seaman and navigator, and at this late stage it would be an unnecessary insult to cast doubt on his word.

I stared through the glasses again, searching this time for the dark sail of the *Yellow Lotus*. I couldn't find it, and for a moment I was baffled. I could hear the steady bleeping of the homing signal coming from the wheelhouse and so I knew that she had to be close. I searched again, and suddenly picked up a light that was blinking only half a mile ahead. I focussed the glasses and saw the outline of a junk's hull and the raking slant of a mast. It had to be our quarry and she had lowered her sail. I hastily ordered Feng to do the same, and heard the quick rush of feet, the creak of ropes and the descending rustle of canvas behind me. The *Sea Pearl* lost way but I kept my eyes glued through the binoculars on to the junk ahead.

The light that the *Yellow Lotus* was now displaying helped me to hold on to her position, and after a moment I realized that she was signalling to the smaller lights that had flickered earlier. I waited and watched, straining my eyes into the darkness. The black waves made the only sound, and I had to brace my legs against the rocking movement as they lifted the deck beneath my feet. Feng waited patiently at my shoulder, and I could sense the other three men also waiting behind my back. Several minutes passed before I was able to work out the logical meaning of the cluster of smaller lights converging upon the one main mastlight of the *Yellow Lotus*.

"She has made a rendezvous with a small fleet of sampans," I said at last.

"For what purpose?" Feng asked.

"I would think that they plan to make a transfer of their cargo." I spoke with satisfaction, for I was convinced that I had now located one of the two vital missing links in the narcotics chain. "If I am right the sacks of opium will be passed over to the sampans, and exchanged for boxes of fish. The police suspect the Cheng-Weng junks of smuggling opium, so the *Yellow Lotus* will return to Castle Bay with only fish in her holds. The small sampans are not capable of sailing all the way to the China coast on the far side of the Pearl River, and so they are not suspected. They will return to their own home port, and they will smuggle the opium over these last few miles into Hong Kong."

"It is a good idea," Feng said, as though the actual act of deceiving the police met with at least some of his approval.

"It is a good idea because they are very clever people," I said slowly. It seemed like a good time to deliver a warning and so I added: "These very clever people are also very dangerous. If they should ever find out that the *Sea*

Pearl has followed one of their junks on its round voyage, then they will kill me, and they will kill you, Captain Feng, and they will kill the three men of your crew." I paused blandly to meet the sudden, startled look in his eyes. "Do you understand that it will not be wise to talk of any of this when we return to Hong Kong?"

Feng looked uncertain, but then he nodded slowly.

"I understand. I will not talk — and neither will my men."

"Good," I smiled and gave his shoulder a friendly squeeze. "That will be the safest way for us all."

★ ★ ★

It was four more hours before the transfer operation was completed. The *Sea Pearl* lay hove to with her sea anchor dragging just over a half mile back from all the activity, and throughout all that time I stood in the bows and watched. Most of the lights went out once the sampan fleet had grouped around the distant *Yellow Lotus*, and all the night-blurred movements were suggested rather than seen. I used the binoculars frequently, but it was all too dark and far away for me to register any actual details. I knew that the milling sampans and the junk were there, and I knew that there could only be one reason for their secret rendezvous, and that was all.

I was scanning the scene at five minute intervals, and was due to raise my binoculars for what must have been at least the eighty-seventh time, when Feng gave me prior warning that the *Yellow Lotus* was again under way. After four days and five nights his hearing was so well attuned to the homing signal that he could judge almost immediately when it began to strengthen or fade. I checked with the binoculars and dimly saw the outline of the large sail hoisted once more to catch the breeze. The *Yellow Lotus* was indeed sailing and pulling away from the scattered smudges that marked the bobbing sampans.

"Must we continue to follow the bleep?" Feng enquired.

I shook my head. "We follow the opium, and now the opium is aboard the sampans."

I went into the wheelhouse and switched off the receiver. The bleeping stopped and the red light went out. The black box had worked well, but now it would only confuse.

"The junk will return to Castle Peak Bay," I said positively. "But I think that the sampan fleet must belong to another home port. Pull in your anchor and then raise up the small forward sail only to match the speed of the sampans."

Feng nodded and gave the necessary orders, while I returned to the blunt bows to keep watch and guide our new course. The tall mainsail of the *Yellow Lotus* had already been swallowed up into the darkness, carrying home her innocent cargo of fish. The smaller vessels, almost a score of them, looking too scattered and dilapidated to be guilty of any co-ordinated plan or movement, continued with the illegal cargo at a slower pace.

We trailed the sampan fleet until my eyes literally ached. More and more junks and sampans began to appear as we neared the shore, most of them fishing harmlessly, and finally I felt that it was safe to let the *Sea Pearl* close in to a quarter of a mile. After that it was easier, but I was not sorry when at long last the low black line of hills that was the New Territories appeared ahead. The sampan fleet had by-passed the wide mouth of Castle Peak, as I had been sure that they would, and continued to follow the shoreline to the east.

After half an hour they began to close together and converge upon a small inlet, one that appeared to be jammed with sampans only, which meant that it must be too shallow to harbour a deep sea junk. We followed in their wake until Feng reluctantly ordered the foresail down and allowed the *Sea Pearl* to drift. He looked at me and shrugged his shoulders to indicate that he could go no further.

I realized that from here I would again have to resort to swimming.

14

I TOLD Feng that he could now take the *Sea Pearl* back to her normal anchorage in the typhoon shelter, and that I would seek him out later to square up our account. He raised no objections and so after shaking hands all round I parted company with Captain and crew and once more slipped over the junk's side into the sea. They gave me a final wave, and then hoisted up the foresail and turned slowly for Kowloon. I swam swiftly to the shore.

I landed a few minutes later to the left of the darkened bay that had by now totally absorbed the slow-moving fleet of sampans, and immediately began to move off on a diagonal course to my right. Above the narrow sand beach I stumbled into a rice field and waded ankle-deep through muddy water and young rice shoots to cut off the corner. Then the ground sloped up for fifty yards, and then down again, bringing me up to the edge of the bay which was no more than the mouth of an inlet capable of packing in less than a hundred sampans. Most of the flat-bottomed boats were in darkness, but at the inward end of the bay there were flickers of light from moving torches and oil lamps. I stayed back from the waters edge, hunched almost double in the black shadow of the low hill, and moved silently in the direction of the milling lights.

As I drew closer to the scene I dropped down on to my belly and wormed my way cautiously over the cold earth. There was very little natural cover, but the darkness made a comfortable shroud. I stopped when I was near enough to distinguish the individual sampans that were now floating around a narrow finger of rotting jetty which looked as though it could collapse at any moment. There were guiding lights on the jetty, and a handful of boatmen were busily catching lines from the sampans and making them secure. At the landward end of the jetty an old canvas-hooded truck was waiting.

I eased myself into a natural hollow in the ground, and then lay perfectly still to watch. There was a foul smell nearby and I had the feeling that I had wriggled my way through something unmentionable, but these were discomforts that I had to ignore. I was interested in the truck, a big old Ford that was now less than thirty yards away. The cab faced towards me, and for a moment I concentrated on memorizing the barely distinguishable letters of the registration number. Then I looked back to the jetty and saw that the first of the sampans had been drawn in close. One of the boatmen helped a passenger up on to the jetty, and as she threw back her head to let her dark shawl fall on to her shoulders I again recognized May Ling. Her smooth, classically beautiful face, was calm and clear in the lamplight.

She walked up the jetty and two men moved from the shadow thrown by the parked truck to meet her. They were two prosperous looking Chinese wearing smart business suits. Both of them were fat and I noticed that one of them flashed gold teeth. May Ling greeted them with a warm smile and offered them her hand in turn. They were obviously old friends, but their exchange of words was too low for me to overhear. They turned and came closer, and I received a mild surprise as a third man moved uncertainly from the dark shadows at the back of the truck. He was a small man with a shaven head and the simple yellow robe and sandals of a Buddhist monk. He bowed slowly to May Ling, and placed the palms of his hands respectfully together in his own gesture of greeting.

May Ling smiled at him, and this time her words carried clearly.

"Hello, Bhikku, we bring you more fish for the poor."

The old priest murmured an answer I could not hear, and bowed the white dome of his head more humbly. The two well-dressed Chinese laughed. After that the formalities were over and May Ling gave brief orders. The canvas flaps at the back of the truck were thrown open and the transfer of the opium began.

For half an hour I watched the sacks of opium being heaved up from the sampans to the jetty, and then being carried almost at a run to the waiting truck. The heavy work was again undertaken by gangs of boatmen and coolies, while May Ling stood aside with her two friends and the silent priest and supervised. I noticed that despite all the lights and the activity there was no show of interest from the silent craft that lay at permanent anchor all around the shallow bay. Obviously all the boat people who lived here knew exactly what was happening, and they must also know that it was wiser to neither observe nor interfere.

When I began to get the cramp I decided that I too had seen enough, and eased myself slowly back into the night. This time I took care not to back into any prowling guard, but it seemed that May Ling and her friends at this end were not as cautious as the old Kuomintang General had been. There was no sign of any roaming patrol to cause me any alarm.

When it was safe to straighten up I began to circle inland, and eventually struck a road that was not much more than a raised earth track through the ricefields. I followed it back warily until I could crouch down within sight of the truck and the jetty again, and after a few minutes I picked out a second vehicle which had previously been shielded from my view. It was a large black saloon car, and was presumably the property of the two Chinese businessmen.

I stared thoughtfully at the black

saloon, toying with dubious ideas such as hiding myself in the back or in the boot. My problem now was to follow the truck when it departed with the opium, and the saloon car was the only other vehicle available. Those risky ideas tempted me, but after five minutes a match suddenly flared inside the car and I saw briefly the face and peaked cap of the chauffeur as he lit himself a cigarette behind the wheel. That was enough to make me realize that I had been on the point of pushing my luck too far, and once more I made a stealthy and silent retreat.

When I was safely out of sight and hearing I turned my back on all the activity in the inlet and began to walk briskly along the only road. I could not hope to follow the opium-laden truck on foot, and it made poor sense to jeopardise all that I had already learned by acting rashly at this stage. My best hope now was to find the main road, and then with luck a town and a telephone so that I could call up either Belinda or Sunny to support me with a car. On either side of me the rice fields gleamed dimly like black lakes in the starlight, and beyond them there was nothing but darkness. I made one effort to make better time with a jogging run, but the track was rutted and stony, and the cut toes of my bruised right foot soon began to cause me pain. I was forced to slow down again to a hurrying walk.

My luck had run out, for it was a long walk to the main road. I made about two and a half miles, and then from behind me I heard the approaching roar of engines in the night. I looked back to see two double beams of headlights swinging round a slight curve, and then I ran off the track for twenty yards into the rice field before I threw myself flat. The muddy water was almost deep enough to cover me and I risked raising my head to watch the two vehicles go past.

The black saloon car was in the lead with the chauffeur at the wheel. May

Ling sat beside him, awake but relaxed, while the two Chinese businessmen occupied the back seat. Next came the old Ford truck, bouncing and jolting even more erratically than the car. I couldn't see the driver's face, but sitting in the cab beside him was the old priest. There could be no doubt about that shaven head and the yellow robe.

After they had gone I stood up slowly, once more dripping wet and stained with mud. I splashed my way back to the raised track and watched the red tail-lights of the two vehicles disappear into the night. Then I resumed walking, although it was now too late to hurry.

★ ★ ★

It was another half mile to the paved road, and then another weary mile before I reached the first small town that was a huddle of poor houses and a few shops. I knocked on one of the shop doors until I succeeded in rousing a frightened old Chinaman, and then I gave him five dollars to compensate for his disturbed sleep and the use of his telephone. He became sympathetic when I told him some polite fiction to the effect that my car had broken down, and that I had accidentally fallen into a rice field in the dark. His wife got up and made me some hot tea, and I was able to wait in the shop until the black Mercedes arrived to collect me. By then I felt obliged to add another five dollars for their hospitality.

Belinda was at the wheel of my car, and Tracey was in the passenger seat beside her. It was only when I got in behind them that I realized that Ralph Slater had also come along for the ride. The two girls had twisted to face me, but almost immediately their delicate nostrils wrinkled in unison.

"David," Tracey said tactlessly, "you do smell — "

" — of the sea — " Belinda tried to be polite.

" — and other things," Tracey

concluded doubtfully.

"I've had a busy time," I said apologetically.

"How busy? What's happened?" Slater didn't give a damn about my perfume. He just wanted to know facts.

I waited until the car was under way, and while Belinda drove us back into Kowloon I gave them all the full story. The tale lasted for the full drive, and after we had parked the car and taken the Star Ferry back to Hong Kong-side, Slater insisted that we all come up to his hotel and finish it off over a drink.

When the girls were firmly established behind gin and tonics and Slater and I had a whisky each the discussion continued.

"It's a pity that you couldn't follow that truck and the old priest," Slater said regretfully. "What did you say they called him?"

"May Ling greeted him as Bhikku," I said calmly. "But it's not a name. It's a title which roughly means just priest — it doesn't mean anything at all."

"Even so, there can't be too many Bhuddist priests in Hong Kong."

"You'd be surprised," I dissented mildly. "We have quite a number of temples and monasteries of one denomination or another. Most of them are so small that a stranger barely notices them."

Slater scowled. "But you got the registration number of that truck, and of the car?"

I nodded. "I fixed them in my memory — but I won't be surprised if it turns out that both those vehicles had false registration plates. Remember that these people are not stupid."

"How do you find out?"

"I don't," I said calmly. "I hand it to the police and let them check it out. They have easier access to the records, and in any case I think that it's high time we called them in."

"No," Slater said quickly. "I don't want the police in — not yet anyway."

"This sounds like the new beginning of an old conversation." I smiled pleasantly as I spoke but I watched his eyes. "Why don't you want the police, Ralph?"

"Because we're so damned close." He set his whisky down and leaned forward to bang his right fist in his left palm. "We've nearly cracked this whole thing ourselves, David, and there's nothing to stop us from going all the way. You've already filled in all the answers except one. We now know that there's a bunch of old diehard Kuomintang soldiers running opium from Yunnan and the golden triangle down through Kwantung province. We know that from there the Cheng-Weng junks are running it along the China coast into Hong Kong waters where the shallow-draught sampans ferry it for the last few miles. Then there's the one missing link, but we do know that before Mr. Shing was killed the opium was almost certainly being smuggled out again as heroin by the Happy

Valley Fruit Company."

He paused, staring at me almost desperately. "That one missing link is the heroin factory, David — the stop between the sampans and the Happy Valley Fruit Company where the opium gets refined into the hard stuff for reshipment. Once we locate the factory then we know everything, and that old monk must be a good enough lead to enable you to find it!"

"Maybe," I said. "But I'm taking a lot of risks, and the only thing to warrant them now is your complete satisfaction. I'm not sure that that's enough."

"I am paying," he said harshly.

"You paid for Lin Hoi," I said. "And then for Mr. Shing. It's got a long way beyond that!"

He tightened his lips, and then decided that I needed another explanation.

"Look, David, I don't know what the cops are like here — but back home you couldn't exactly accuse the police force of being incorruptible. I could take something as solid as this to the cops back home and somewhere in that police building there would be someone who would make damn sure that the whole thing got screwed up. Now I don't want to say that maybe it's the same way here, and that maybe one of your Hong Kong cops is on the payroll of this narcotics syndicate, but at the same time I don't want to take that chance. I just want to be sure that when we do go to the police this business will be stitched up so tight that nobody can pull it apart and kick the pieces under the carpet."

It was a well-put argument, with just the right amount of doubtful anguish, and so I nodded as though he had convinced me.

"Okay, Ralph, if that's how you feel we'll give it another couple of days and try to sew up the loose ends. But after that, whether we find the old monk or not, I'm going to have to take this to the police."

Slater smiled, and looked relieved.

"That's fine with me. If you give yourself two days then I reckon that will be enough. The progress you've made so far gives me a kind of blind faith in your abilities."

I smiled at that and then finished my whisky.

"Now I'd better go. It's late, and I'm badly in need of a bath."

"You can use my bathroom." Slater looked embarrassed, as though only now did he realize that he had played a poor host.

"Thanks," I said. "But I need a change of clothes too. It's time I got home anyway."

Tracey and Belinda dutifully finished their gin and tonics, and then we all said goodnight and left.

★ ★ ★

I took the two girls home with me, and told them to fix themselves fresh drinks while I took a brief shower. I rejoined them after ten minutes, scrubbed down, deodorized, and wearing a blue silk bathrobe and slippers. They unanimously applauded the improvement. I topped them up with more gin, poured myself another whisky, and then we all made ourselves comfortable.

"Now tell me about yourselves," I said. I looked to Tracey. "When did you get back from Macau?"

"Only a few hours ago. I stayed there the full five days and then caught the hydrofoil back this afternoon."

"Did you get that double bill?"

She nodded, and opened her handbag to hand me the receipted bill made out in my name for two single rooms for five days at the Chinese Palace Hotel. "Mr. Soong sends it with his compliments," she said calmly. From the depths of her bag she pulled out three typewritten sheets stapled together and added, "This comes with mine."

I flipped through the pages while she explained.

"Mr. Shing did stay in Macau

258

between the dates May Ling specified. He booked a room at the August Moon Hotel. During his stay he gambled at most of the casinos, but most of his time he spent on the lower deck of the floating casino in the inner harbour. His favourite game was fan tan. That's the one where the croupier cuts a cupful of beans out of a pile and then withdraws the remainder four at a time. The players bet on whether there will be three, two, one or no beans left after the last complete four are pulled away. The odds are not unreasonable, and Mr. Shing seemed to prefer it to the roulette table or the card games. As far as I can tell he broke even. It's all in my report."

I closed the pages of the report and smiled at her.

"Thanks, Tracey. This should at least satisfy May Ling."

She shrugged. "It has no other value. It's obvious now that May Ling only wanted you in Macau so that you wouldn't be aware of her own absence from Hong Kong."

"And with this she'll believe that she got what she wanted." I smiled because I didn't want her to disparage her own work. "This is a card in our favour."

Tracey frowned as though she was not impressed, so I turned to Belinda who had been sitting patiently with her gin and tonic.

"How about you? Is there anything to report on Slater?"

Belinda nodded, and her face was unusually serious.

"Yes, David, there is. I've allowed Ralph to take me out to dinner twice, but he hasn't let anything slip. However, what he doesn't know is that I've also been watching him through Sunny, and some of Sunny's friends from the gym. They've reported back that Ralph has recently made some new friends of his own. He's been meeting with two hard-case Americans who call themselves Jay Fletcher and Chuck Rennick. I can't find out much about them, except that they've only recently arrived in Hong Kong and that they are staying at a cheap hotel. What disturbs me is that this morning Sunny phoned in again to say that Fletcher and Rennick have been busy recruiting a rather nasty bunch of the local Chinese hoodlums." She paused. "What I cannot understand is what does Ralph Slater want with a gang of thugs?"

"I have a feeling that we shall soon find out," I said calmly. "Slater keeps pushing us on, and at the same time finding objections every time I mention the police. Now I've given him only two more days, so in that time he's got to show his hand."

"You mean that we just wait for him to pick his moment?" Belinda said doubtfully.

I nodded. "We'll leave Sunny to keep a long-distance watch on Slater and his new friends, while we concentrate on finding this renegade priest. The important thing is to remember that Slater does have his own motives, and that we are moving on very dangerous ground. We tread gently and play everything by ear and by instinct, and you girls make no moves at all without my knowledge and approval."

They both chose to pout at me to express their displeasure, and so I took advantage and kissed each pair of shapely lips in turn. "Now go home and go to bed," I told them, "because I have to get some sleep."

They went, but I didn't get any sleep. The telephone rang five minutes later, and when I picked it up I heard the softly seductive voice of May Ling.

15

I LOOKED at my wristwatch and realized that it was already eight o'clock in the morning. May Ling sounded drowsy and comfortable over the phone and I suspected that she was just awake and yawning.

"Hello, David," she said sweetly. "I thought you should be back from Macau by now. I hope that I haven't called you too early."

"Not at all," I answered just as agreeably. "As it happens I'm already out of bed. We private detectives always have a busy day."

"How sad," she sympathized lazily. "I am still in my bed. Have you had breakfast yet?"

"Not yet."

"Then why don't you come over and join me. We can talk over coffee and you can tell me about Macau."

"That sounds just fine. I'll be right over."

I heard her soft laugh and imagined her smile, and then she rang off. I put down the receiver and stifled a yawn of my own, and then wearily I refolded my pyjamas and put them back under my pillow. I switched off the light and then drew the curtains to verify reluctantly that it was indeed daylight. Then I got dressed in a white shirt and tie and a pale blue suit. I postponed sleep until another time and went out to catch the Star Ferry back to Kowloon.

When I knocked on the door of the apartment in Empress Building it was opened by a young Chinese girl. She bowed shyly to avoid my eyes and then led me immediately through the small kitchen and into the large bedroom. May Ling was still relaxed in her bed, with her pillows propped up behind her and a silver breakfast tray fitted like a low table over the coverlet. She smiled as she invited me inside, and dismissed her maid with a brief sign of her hand.

"I am a very idle person," she said, not making an apology but stating a fact. "I always rise late, and I always take my breakfast in bed."

"The sun is beautiful whenever it rises," I said blandly.

She smiled as she set down her coffee cup, and carefully she patted her ripe lips with a napkin.

"For that compliment you may kiss me."

She leaned back on her pillows and I kissed her with what I considered to be just the right amount of pressure, neither dissenting nor demanding. My hands lingered for a moment on the smooth nakedness of her shoulders, and I did nothing to hide my awareness of the low cut froth of transparent nightdress that only partially concealed her breasts. When I drew away she was still smiling, and I had to concede that for a woman who had spent the last five days skulking in junks and sampans on the South China Seas, she did play the idle courtesan remarkably well.

"Would you like coffee now?" she asked calmly.

I nodded, and she carefully poured me a cup of coffee from the silver pots on her tray. She gave me the cup, and then lifted the cover from a silver salver to reveal half a dozen rashers of crisp bacon and four fried eggs.

"Would you like to eat?"

I was famished, but it did not seem to be a good idea to let her suspect that I too had spent the night working up an appetite. I declined tactfully.

"Thank you, but no, at the moment I am not hungry."

"Then I will eat later. Please lift the tray away."

I did as she asked and then sat on the edge of the bed. We both sipped coffee for a moment, and then she came to the point.

"Tell me about your trip to Macau, David? When did you return to Hong Kong?"

"Yesterday afternoon," I lied easily.

"And you did not call me immediately?"

She raised her eyebrows in a mock frown, but I scented a subtle trap. Knowing that she had been away I could have pretended that I had called in her absence, but I suspected that her maid had probably been on hand at all times to answer the door and telephone and give excuses for her mistress. May Ling almost certainly knew that I had not made any attempts to contact her over the past five days, and she was probably wondering why.

"I intended to call as soon as I got back," I said calmly. "But I have another client who was waiting for me at the office. I was engaged upon a case for him before I left for Macau, and he was somewhat angry that I had allowed his business to lapse. It was a stormy interview that lasted for the rest of the afternoon. When my client finally left my office it was time to close down. So I decided that I would call you today." I smiled. "But you called first."

Her eyes twinkled. "Was your client very annoyed?"

"Very."

"But you preferred to look for Mr. Shing. I am grateful. Who was your other client?"

I shook my head gently. "You shouldn't ask. We private detectives are like doctors, we are not supposed to discuss the details of other cases. It's a matter of professional ethics."

She smiled but didn't press the matter. She was assuming that the angry client to whom I referred must be Ralph Slater, and so she was satisfied.

"What did you learn about poor Mr. Shing?"

"Quite a lot." I reached inside my jacket and drew out the three-page report that Tracey had compiled and typed. "I've found evidence that Mr. Shing did spend some of his time in Macau, and that he did frequent the gambling houses. He seems to have spent most of his gambling time on the lower deck of the floating casino.

He had a preference for fan tan, but as far as I can ascertain he did not lose a great deal of money." I gave her the report. "This is a list of his movements during his stay. I worked on it for five days, so I am convinced that it is complete."

May Ling took the list and studied it for a moment. "He stayed at the August Moon Hotel," she observed. "Did you also stay there?"

"No. Miss Ryan and I stayed at the Chinese Palace Hotel." It was a perfect opening to show her the double bill. "I am afraid that this must go on to your account, together with the hydrofoil tickets."

She looked at the bill briefly. "Two single rooms, I am surprised at you David Chan! I would have thought that Miss Ryan would be most desirable, and a double room so much cheaper."

"Miss Ryan is very desirable," I agreed. "But I have an excellent working relationship with both my partners, and intimacy with either one would spoil it. Besides, I also find you very desirable, and it would have been crude of me to share a double room with another woman while you were footing the bill."

She laughed. "David, I think that in some ways you are as devious as you are handsome. But you are right, I am happy to pay for two single rooms."

She returned the bill, and raised her lips to be kissed. Again I complied.

"But what about Mr. Shing," she asked when she drew back. "Do you still have no clue as to what might have happened to him?"

I allowed professional gloom to descend upon my face.

"I have traced all his movements in Macau, but there is nothing to suggest that he left Macau with any heavy gambling debts. I fear that we must resume searching for clues to his disappearance here in Hong Kong." I paused hopefully. "Have you learned anything new while I have been away?"

She began to look distressed and

shook her head. "There has been nothing. I have waited by the telephone, hoping that he will call. I have waited for the postman, hoping that he will write. Every day I have telephoned the Happy Valley Fruit Company, hoping that they have received some message. And every day I have visited his apartment in Paradise Building in the hope that he may have returned. All my hopes have been in vain. Either he is hiding somewhere, or he is dead."

Her eyes were wet and she turned her face away. Gently I rested my hand on her bare arm.

"Do you want me to continue searching?"

She looked up at me and nodded weepily. "Yes please, David, search for a little while longer. I do not think that you will find him now, but I must do all that I can."

I waited for a moment while she found a small handkerchief to dab her brimming eyes. Then I said quietly:

"But where shall I search? There were no clues at his apartment, and none at his place of business, and none in Macau. You must think, and give me some more ideas — somewhere else to start."

She didn't disappoint me. She nodded uncertainly and leaned out of bed to reach a small bedside table. She pulled open the single drawer and removed a sheet of paper which she offered for my inspection.

"While you have been away I have had time to think. I knew that if you found nothing in Macau then you would have to start again here in Hong Kong. To help you I have made this list of all the places I know that were favourite with Mr. Shing. Most of them are nightclubs and bars, although some of them are gambling places. Perhaps — perhaps if you visit them all and ask questions?"

I smiled, for the list was a long one, which was very much as I had expected. To check them all out would take several days, and would leave me no time to work on the Slater case. She was still buying me off with a softer job, and no doubt hoping that Slater would eventually pack up and go home in disgust. When that happened and my retainer went with him, she would assume that I too would be only too happy to drop the dangerous narcotics investigation. For the moment the advantage was mine if I pretended to play along.

"I'll go to them all," I assured her. "And I'll question every bartender and hostess and doorman. I'm sure that we must learn something."

She looked relieved, and just in case she realized that it was all going too easy I threw in a blunt question to rattle her. "There's just one point," I said. "If Mr. Shing does prove to be dead, then who is his beneficiary? Who gets his money, and who becomes the new owner of the Happy Valley Fruit Company?"

She looked embarrassed. "I do,

David. Mr. Shing recently made a will leaving everything to me." She paused, looked up horrified, and shot me the old dramatic line that she had obviously polished up in anticipation of this moment. "But, David, surely you don't think — "

She paused in just the right place and I patted her arm gently. It was my turn to be trite.

"Of course not. I just wanted to be sure so that I could eliminate that possibility."

"Thank you, David." She looked relieved again.

I glanced at my wristwatch, and then at the list of nightclubs she had given me. "I'd better get a move on. It's time I was paying attention to the job and started checking on some of these addresses."

"Wait, David," she reached for my arm. "Most of them will not be open until noon. You do not have to go yet."

I looked into her dark, slanted

almond eyes, and then at the alluring curves of that aroused female body that her flimsy nightdress so blatantly offered and revealed. I remembered that her favours and my seduction were all part of the deal to keep me happy, and so when she smiled, I smiled also. She began to unfasten my collar and loosen my tie, and so for the next hour or two I permitted her to keep me happy.

I must admit that there are times when I really do enjoy my work.

* * *

It was 1 p.m. when I finally arrived at the office, and I found Belinda holding the fort alone with only a sandwich and a glass of milk to sustain her. She looked up from her desk as I entered.

"Did you have a good morning in bed?" she enquired politely.

I was almost lost for an answer until I recalled that when we had parted five hours before I had been proclaiming my firm intention of getting into my own bed for a much-needed sleep.

"A very good morning," I said, and tried hard to look like a man who had slept well and chaste. I wasn't sure that I succeeded, and so I changed the subject. "Where's Tracey?"

"She went out with Sunny to find your Captain Feng and the *Sea Pearl*. Your parting instructions didn't leave us a lot of scope, and rather than just waste time waiting for you to wake up we decided that she could pay off Feng and collect our homing receiver and your binoculars."

"Good thinking," I approved. "Did you ask Sunny to retrieve the bug he planted on the *Yellow Lotus*?"

She nodded. "He promised to see to it."

"So all we have to do now is to get on with finding one little man with a shaven head and a yellow robe."

Belinda smiled. "I think it's possible that I've already found him. I haven't been idle while you've been snoring."

"You've what!" I stared at her and almost exploded.

"Now calm down, David." Her hazel eyes gave me a stern, schoolmistress freeze through her spectacles. "I didn't have to take any kind of risk. I didn't even leave the office. I just made one telephone call."

I sat down and relaxed. "Okay, I apologize. Who did you call?"

"The Chartered Bank."

I looked at her blankly and waited.

"May Ling paid you the usual advance retaining fee," Belinda explained. "The cheque was made out on the Chartered Bank. Obviously she has an account there, so I simply rang them up this morning, identified myself as Miss May Ling, and asked for a statement of my account. The clerk didn't suspect that I wasn't May Ling and read me the statement to date. Do you realize, David, that your charming little paramour is rich to the tune of over one million HK dollars?"

I whistled wryly, and then asked. "What else?"

Belinda smiled. "I pretended to be surprised. I said that I had believed that there was more than that. The clerk was most obliging, he read me back the entries of the last few withdrawals to suggest where I might be mistaken. One was that miserable little cheque that she paid to us, the other, he reminded me, was my regular five-thousand dollars monthly subscription to the Golden Light Monastery!"

I whistled again. "So May Ling makes regular donations to a monastery. That's out of character with a woman who smuggles narcotics, so my sense of logic concludes that those donations must be pay cheques to our renegade priest."

Belinda nodded. "My sense of logic reached the same conclusion, so I checked up the location of the Golden Light Monastery. You will be amazed to learn that it is situated in the New Territories, only five miles from that

278

inlet where the sampans landed last night, and less than a mile from the spot where we picked you up."

"That settles it," I said firmly, "the Golden Light Monastery will most definitely bear investigation."

16

TO approach the monastery we needed the cover of darkness, so in the meantime I took Belinda out to a late lunch. When we returned Tracey was still absent. I put my feet up on my desk and dozed for an hour, hoping that she would come in. She didn't, and finally I wrote her a short note of explanation and propped it on her desk against her typewriter. I thought carefully after that, and then I picked up the telephone and dialled Ralph Slater's hotel number. He was at home, and sounded positively eager when he recognized my voice.

"Hi, David, you're up and about sooner than I expected. What's new?"

"I think I've found that missing link," I said calmly. "Or rather my clever Belinda has found it for me. She had the bright idea of checking up on May Ling's bank account, and discovered that May Ling makes regular donations to a Buddhist monastery out in the New Territories. I'm convinced that it must tie up, so we're heading out there to take a look. I thought maybe you'd care to come along?"

"Hell, David — too damn right I want to come along! Just hold back a minute and I'll be right over."

"I thought that's how you'd feel," I spoke placidly and winked one eye at the dubious Belinda. "That's why I gave you a call."

"Thanks, David. I knew I could rely on you. No more talk now. I'm on my way."

I heard his phone click and replaced my own receiver more gently. "Our friend Ralph is on his way," I told Belinda.

"Are you sure that's wise, David?" She was frowning and obviously doubting my sanity.

"I'm not at all sure," I admitted. "But the only way to find out what

Ralph Slater is really after is to deal the cards and let him play out his hand."

"And then what?" Belinda demanded practically.

I opened my desk drawer and took out the 9 mm Chinese automatic. "All I need," I said blandly, "is one trump card."

I stood up, removed my jacket, and slipped on the shoulder holster and harness.

★ ★ ★

When Slater arrived I shut up the office and we departed for the New Territories. Once on Kowloon-side I picked up my black Mercedes and took the wheel, while Belinda navigated beside me. Slater took the back seat and I filled him in with the minor details during the hour-long drive. He sat forward tensely, with his grey eyes and knuckle-hammered face filling my driving mirror. His big hands gripped the back of the front seat so hard that the hairy knuckles gleamed white, and I noticed that on his shirt cuffs he wore the same heavy gold cufflinks that he had worn when we first met. I remembered the Colt 0.45 that had been pointed at me on that occasion, and guessed that he too was again wearing a shoulder holster.

We cleared Kowloon and the industrial town of Tsuen Wan and headed out on the familiar road to Castle Peak Bay. Belinda consulted her map and a few miles before the dirt road to the unmarked inlet where the sampan fleet had landed she told me to slow down. A similar dirt road appeared on our right, leading away from the sea and through more ricefields into the central hills.

"That's the way," Belinda said quietly. "It's about a mile and a half to the monastery."

"And about half an hour to darkness," I added, looking along the coastline to where the sun was setting into the sea. I turned the wheel away from the sunset and eased the car on to the dirt road running inland.

I drove slowly, and when at last we came in sight of the Golden Light Monastery there were only a few fading minutes of daylight left. It was just enough to get a brief idea of the layout of the place, which was all that I needed. The monastery was situated on a low hill rising out of the flat plain of surrounding rice fields. Only the slanting roofs of the temple and flanking pavilions showed above a high surrounding wall, the green tiles reflecting the last rays of dying light. Set into the wall was a chinese-style gateway with more green tiles and green-painted iron gates. Tree tops showed above the walls, suggesting cool gardens in the temple grounds. Outside the wall to the left were a few small outbuildings, some low huts and animal pens.

I wound down my window and tested the light breeze that was blowing across the low valley.

"Smells like they keep pigs or chickens over there."

Slater had also caught the faint scent on the wind, and I turned to him and nodded.

"That's right, Ralph. When opium is refined into heroin it has to be steamed. There's a distinctive smell, and so the oldest trick in the book is to site your heroin factory beside a farmyard where the natural animal smells can mask any escaping fumes from the opium."

"So you're really sure that this is the right place?"

"It's an ideal location," I said cautiously. "And everything points to it being the right place."

"So what now?"

"Now I have to take a closer look, just to confirm," I said calmly. "It's nearly dark so Belinda and I will take a walk over there and check it out. The only problem is that if another vehicle comes down this road to approach the monastery, then our own car parked here will be a dead giveaway." I paused

285

and turned in my seat. "Ralph, would you mind taking the car back to the main road. Give us an hour and then drive up here again to look for us. If we're not on our way out — then you'd better call in the police."

I expected him to argue, or at least to insist that he should be the one to accompany me while Belinda took the car back. However, this time he surprised me, for after only a momentary hesitation he nodded in agreement.

"Okay, David, but you take it cool and easy."

I smiled. "I always take it cool and easy — it's my natural style."

Belinda and I got out of the car and Slater shifted into the driving seat to take the wheel. He checked his wristwatch, promised to be back in the hour, and then reversed the car along the narrow dirt road. When he was out of sight I turned towards the monastery. Belinda still hesitated with a frown.

"David, that man's keyed up for something like a ticking time bomb, and he fell in with your plans too easily. I don't like letting him out of our sight."

"Neither do I," I admitted. "But I'm giving him room to play his own game. We just have to watch our backs and wait to see what develops."

Belinda pulled her pretty face into a grimace, and then we began to walk the last few hundred yards to the monastery. The shadows had lengthened into night and so we now had the essential cover of darkness. We kept to the road and approached the chinese gateway to the temple grounds. The gates were closed and fastened with a large padlock. There was a bell rope on the adjoining wall but I refrained from giving it a pull. I steered Belinda away to the right.

"We climb over the wall," I said softly.

"You should be wearing a mini-skirt," Belinda complained, but I knew that she would follow me regardless.

The wall was about eight feet high, and by reaching up I could easily grip the top. The old stonework was crumbling and I felt along for a solid section, and then I heaved myself up and froze with my weight on my arms while I looked along the wall for the glint of any booby trap wires. There was nothing and so I swung one leg over the wall and sat astride while I reached down to give Belinda a helping hand. Despite her mini-skirt she was up and over in three easy seconds, and then I dropped down beside her in the temple grounds.

We were in the dark shadows of a tasteful garden of flowering shrubs and camellia trees. The green tiles of the temple and its adjoining pavilions now looked grey, but the slanted roofs and the upward curving eaves made a peaceful silhouette against the brightening starlight. On this side, away from the farmyard pens, there was the faint scent of incense in the air.

We moved away from the wall, closer to the temple complex. The main temple was constructed in the shape of two octagonal buildings with tall columns and twin one-storey pagoda towers raised above the first level of roofs. It faced a small square of cobbled courtyard, and on either side of the courtyard were the two longer pavilions, presumably the living quarters and schoolrooms for the monks. There was an atmosphere of peacefully crumbling age. Some of the roof tiles needed repair and parts of the gardens were overgrown. There was silence and no sign of life, but standing in the courtyard was a familiar old Ford truck with a hooped canvas hood.

"I recognize the truck," I told Belinda softly. "It's the same vehicle that loaded up the opium from the sampans last night."

I needed no more confirmation, but having come this far I was prepared to investigate all the way. I signed to Belinda to keep close behind me, and then circled silently through the camellia trees behind the right hand pavilion. We approached the courtyard again through the narrow gap between the long pavilion and the main temple, passing beneath a low, ornamental archway.

We waited for several moments in the shadows, but there was no sound to alarm us and no sign of life. There was not even a bird stirring in the gardens. All was still as though the ancient monastery was abandoned, and yet the scent of incense was now stronger. Keeping behind the tall columns I moved silently up the steps to look inside the main temple. A single lamp burned dimly before the altar and the gilded image of the Buddha. Joss sticks burned and embroidered scarlet banners hung motionless against a blurred impression of more gold leaf and red lacquer. Kneeling before the altar was an old monk in his yellow robe, his hands clasped and his shaven head bowed in an attitude of engrossed prayer. His hunched back was towards me, but I knew that this was the same Bhikku whom May Ling had greeted at the sampan jetty.

Belinda was just behind me, and I looked into her eyes and nodded silently to indicate that we had indeed found our renegade priest, and then I crouched low and led her past the temple entrance. In the shadow of the opposite archway that linked to the left hand pavilion we paused.

"This is the closest building to those farm pens outside the perimeter wall," I said softly. "My guess is that the heroin factory must be either inside this pavilion or underneath it."

Belinda nodded in agreement, and we moved to investigate.

The pavilion was raised about four feet above ground level, and we ascended a short flight of steps to the covered verandah. We walked along slowly, keeping in shadow, but all the doors and windows into the building were innocently open, and every room appeared to be empty. At the far end of the verandah we descended to the courtyard again.

"Underneath?" Belinda murmured.

I nodded, and we squeezed behind the verandah steps. The upper walls and roof of the pavilion were constructed of wood, but here there was a four foot base wall of large stone blocks forming the foundations. We moved along cautiously with our heads bowed low beneath the verandah floor. In the gloom I could see nothing except for the occasional chink of starlight through the boards above, but I ran my hand along the cold stone until I found what I expected to find, the hollow recess of a doorway.

I took out my pencil torch, hooded the beam with my hand, and shone it briefly. The low doorway was con- structed solidly of wood and studded heavily with square bolt heads, and it was fastened with another large padlock. I handed the torch to Belinda and she accepted it without comment.

From inside my jacket I took out a small leather wallet containing a selection of hooks, needles and miniature screwdriver blades. I fitted a blunt needle into the socket of the two-inch handle that was part of the kit, and began probing inside the padlock. It was a well-oiled lock that had been frequently used and it took me two minutes to click it open.

I closed up my lock-picking kit and gave it to Belinda in exchange for my torch.

"If somebody comes along and finds this door open it will be another dead giveaway," I said softly. "So you'll have to stay behind. Close the door, and if anyone does approach snap the padlock and back away. You can always open it again the same way that I did."

She nodded reluctantly. "I'll keep watch, you be careful."

I smiled at her in the gloom, and then pushed open the heavy wooden door. A flight of stone steps led downwards, disappearing into unseen bowels of blackness. I descended the first three steps and Belinda closed the door behind me, I was alone in total, musty darkness.

I switched the torch on again and continued slowly down the narrow stairway. The stone steps were smoothly worn, suggesting frequent use, but the trapped air was as still and silent as a grave. I stopped to listen but heard nothing. I breathed deeply, and caught a whiff of ether and the fumes of opium. I had no more doubts, but I continued to the bottom of the steep flight of steps and shone my torch all around.

I realized that I was standing in an extensive network of cellars hewn out below the monastery. Several of the intervening walls had been knocked down and a large floor area cleared to make one vast underground room, with several smaller cellars and alcoves leading off on either side. In one of the side rooms an electric generator had been installed for providing lights and power for the pump and ventilating fans that had been installed to disperse the unavoidable fumes. A large sink unit showed where a clean water supply had been piped down from above, and on the long wooden working tables I recognized all the technical equipment necessary for refining heroin. In one corner a wide chute had been installed, and to one side at the bottom were stacked a hundred or more sacks of raw opium awaiting processing.

There was a sense of satisfaction in finding those sacks, for they had to be the cargo from the *Yellow Lotus*. I passed them and explored slowly. In another side room at the far end of the factory I found stacked boxes of plastic fruits bearing the name of the Happy Valley Fruit Company. I didn't have to open one to know that this time every fruit would be a container for one or perhaps two ounces of pure heroin. On a nearby bench fitted out with well balanced scales and stainless steel scoops and trowels, were large deep trays of the extracted white death, all ready to be measured out and packed in turn.

I had seen enough and I turned away. It had been a long trail; from Lin Hoi to Mr. Shing, from the Happy Valley Fruit Company to Cheng-Weng Junks, and finally through May Ling to the Golden Light monastery. Now I had uncovered it all, and this was the final link. All I had to do was to collect Belinda and get out. I got half way back to the flight of stone steps, and then I heard the soft foot-fall behind me.

I crouched low, and spun round fast in the same moment that a switch clicked down and the whole of the underground factory was flooded with a bright white light. I didn't get the chance to see who was responsible for that action, for I was in more immediate danger from the determined Chinese with a gun who was coming up fast behind me. Fortunately the sudden shock of light proved as blinding for him as for me. He paused to blink while I was still sweeping round by instinct and I flung out my right arm automatically in a straight, stiff-palmed chop that sent pain crashing through my fingers, but at the same time knocked the gun spinning from his hand.

In the same moment I realized that he had at least one friend, for a second man sprang on to my unprotected back. Caught by surprise and with the momentum of my own swing still pitching me forward I dropped to my knees. I arched my back and heaved as I fell on to my face, but I couldn't get enough strength behind it to pitch him off. He slithered higher up my back and locked an arm around my throat. I squirmed desperately and wriggled myself round to face his chest. I braced both hands on the stone floor, kicked up my legs to balance on a hand-stand, and then straightened both arms and legs with a violent upward thrust that broke me clear of the stranglehold and left my opponent looking baffled. I bounded upright and wheeled to face his friend.

The first man had failed to find his gun but in it's place he had grabbed up the nearest weapon to hand, a bright steel spanner which he swung in a vicious blow at my head, I ducked, straightened up a split second after the whizzing spanner had brushed my hair, and deftly caught his lunging arm. I twisted, heaved, and sent him hurtling head foremost across the floor. His journey ended when the top of his head came into solid contact with the leg of a heavy wooden table. The leg collapsed and the table fell on top of him with a crash of breaking glass from the spilled equipment.

The second man was getting uncertainly to his feet when I hit him with an elbow-jarring right hook that flipped him over backwards, and this time he lay still. I spun round again on my heel, looking for whoever had switched on the lights, but by now I was far too late.

"That is enough, David!" May Ling said hysterically. "I warn you, that is enough."

I heeded her warning, for she had picked up the fallen gun and now held it pointed unerringly at my chest. She wore her red *cheongsam* and looked as sleek and lovely as ever before, but now there was a new light of fury in her eyes. The gun in her hand was another 9 mm Chinese automatic. It was identical to, and reminded me of my own, except that my gun was still in its holster where I couldn't reach it without getting shot.

May Ling advanced slowly. She and her friends had appeared from the opposite side of the cellar where I now saw that there was another flight of stone steps leading up to an open door set halfway up the wall.

"Move backwards, David," she said harshly. "Move back into the alcove behind you."

I looked over my shoulder and then decided that at the moment I had little choice but to obey. I moved in the direction she had indicated and she followed me warily. Her eyes never left my face and I had no chance to jump her. I backed into the low stone archway that had formed an original corner of the old cellars, and as I did so I noticed a large steel lever set in the nearby wall. May Ling reached for the lever and pulled it down hard with her free hand. There was a rumble of sound above my head and I looked up quickly. A heavy iron grating crashed down in front of my face, and effectively sealed off the small alcove into a neat prison cell.

"This place has a long history," May Ling said harshly. "And there have been other curious persons like yourself. This little jail has been used many times."

"Has it always been used by your narcotics syndicate." I enquired calmly. "Or is the history more varied than that?"

The tone of my voice was a

miscalculation, for it had the effect of irritating her even more.

"You are a fool, David Chan," she cried angrily. And she raised the automatic to aim at my heart through the thick bars of the grating. "You are not quite the kind of fool that I thought you were, but you are still a fool! I think that I want to kill you now."

My throat was suddenly dry, but in the same moment there was a movement behind her.

"I wouldn't do that," Belinda Carrington said quietly. "He's quite a nice little chap really."

17

BELINDA had descended the main steps on tip-toe and in stockinged feet, and she was within six feet of May Ling's shoulder when she announced her presence with her few well-chosen words. May Ling was startled, her almond eyes opened wide beneath her slanted brows, and then she turned sharply with the gun in her hand. Belinda was holding one of her shoes by the toe. She swung it deftly and the spiked heel smacked painfully into May Ling's slender wrist and the gun flew from her suddenly nerveless fingers as she yelped with pain.

For a moment then the two girls faced each other, May Ling glaring wildly and rubbing her bruised wrist, while Belinda waited with a faintly enquiring expression on her face. I noticed that Belinda had prudently removed her spectacles and left them behind somewhere with her other shoe.

"Now, Ladies — " I began hopefully.

It was pointless to go any further for in that moment May Ling made up her mind and sprang at Belinda with a curse and all the ferocity of a wounded cat. Belinda gave her an unladylike but typically English punch on the nose before May Ling's attacking weight carried her backwards and then they went down together in a fighting heap.

Trapped behind the iron grating in my cell there was nothing that I could do to interfere. I could only watch and await the outcome, and with four of the most beautiful legs in the world flailing and kicking in tangled combat I might almost have enjoyed it, if only they had not been fighting for my life!

For a few minutes the battle was disorganized and undignified. They simply rolled to and fro across the stone floor, with May Ling striving to claw and bite, and Belinda struggling to get a restraining hold on the more abandoned contortions of her opponent. May Ling emerged on top and it looked as though Belinda was losing. May Ling was sitting astride her and ready to hammer her in the face with both fists. However, the short mini-skirt gave complete freedom of movement to Belinda's long, supple legs. She kicked high, hooked her right ankle around May Ling's throat and dragged her back. She only just failed to lock a scissor-grip around May Ling's neck with her legs, and then by some mutual agreement they both rolled apart and scrambled up to begin again.

By now they were both dishevelled and breathing heavily. May Ling cursed softly in Chinese, but Belinda simply waited for her next attack. May Ling decided to rush in with a straightforward low blow to the stomach with her clenched fist, and that was her mistake. Belinda met her with the approved judo counter to a disembowelling stroke with a knife.

As May Ling's right fist hooked up Belinda blocked the blow with her own left forearm. Her right hand clamped down on May Ling's arm above the elbow, and moving quickly past her she twisted May Ling's arm up and behind her back. May Ling screeched with rage and struggled frantically. She couldn't break the arm lock and only succeeded in causing herself more pain, and so finally she became still and conceded defeat.

Belinda was still panting heavily, but after a moment she pushed her prisoner towards the large lever set in the wall.

"Open the cage," she ordered briefly.

May Ling set her lips and made no effort to comply. Belinda gave her a few seconds and then twisted the trapped arm. May Ling opened her mouth in silent pain and tears came to her eyes. Reluctantly she reached out her free hand and pushed the lever up.

"You have to lift the grating," she winced bitterly. "It is not automatic."

I hooked both hands under the bars

and lifted. I had tried it before and nothing had happened, but this time the grating moved freely. Only the weight made it difficult to raise up. When I had pushed it above my head May Ling released the lever to lock it into position.

I stepped out of the alcove cell and relieved Belinda of the responsibility of holding May Ling. Gently, and almost regretfully, I pushed her into the space I had just vacated. "I think it must be your turn to reside in there," I said, and then I pulled the lever to unlock the grating and let it fall back in place. May Ling stared at me dully through the bars, not at all pleased with our reversed circumstances, and then she turned her back on me and stared silently at the far wall.

I turned my attention to Belinda. She was still regaining her breath and her superb bosom was heaving regularly. Her long, dark hair was slowly taking shape again as she smoothed it back with her hands, and her large hazel eyes looked twice as magnificent without her spectacles. I owed her my life, and that made me emotional. I took her in my arms and kissed her with real feeling.

"Belinda, I love you," I told her simply.

Her eyes blinked rather rapidly before my own, and then I felt the soft lips under mine curving into a warm smile.

"I love you too, David" — she paused there to make a point and then finished, — "like a brother." She returned my kiss more gently, and then drew away.

I released her, knowing that she was right.

"Thanks for coming to my rescue," I said lamely.

"I heard the disturbance," she explained. "So I eased open the door and peeped inside. I could see that all the lights were on so I knew that something was wrong." She glanced around the floor at the two unconscious Chinese whom I had laid low before her arrival. "What shall we do with these?"

"They're May Ling's friends," I said. "I suppose we'd better put them in the cell to join her."

"That's a good idea," a new but familiar voice interrupted grimly. "And when you've done that it would be another good idea if you both stayed in the cell to keep them all company."

Belinda and I both turned and looked up. Ralph Slater was slowly descending the stairs with his Colt 0.45 gripped firmly in his hand. His appearance was not entirely unexpected, and so I was not unduly surprised. Behind him was another tall American with a tough, lean face and blonde hair, and another Colt 0.45. A third American, thick-set and black-haired, and also armed, was prodding ahead of him the terrified figure of the little Bhikkhu in the yellow robe whom they had obviously collected from the temple above. Filling in at the top of the stairs were half a dozen of the local Chinese toughs.

The whole party descended to the floor of the underground dope factory and began to fan out in a half circle. Slater was watching me, and he said warningly:

"Don't try anything, David. I know how smart you are and I know how fast you can move. Even if I was alone I wouldn't let you take me twice." He paused. "Besides, I've got a lot to thank you for. I needed you to find this place, and I'm really sorry that I had to play you for a fool. Now I don't want to have to hurt you. I don't want to have to hurt Belinda. But make no mistake, David — if you push me you'll still be dead."

"No pushing," I agreed, and raised my hands mildly. I looked to his two companions. "Aren't you going to introduce me to your friends, Ralph. I know that one of them is Jay Fletcher and the other is Chuck Rennick, but I don't know which is which."

Slater looked startled. There was a moment of silence, and then the two hardcase Americans exchanged glances. The blonde one decided to speak.

"I'm Chuck Rennick."

I nodded to him amiably. "Tell me, Chuck, did you and Jay hire our mutual friend Ralph — or did Ralph hire you?"

"I hired them!" Slater said harshly. He didn't like the idea of my questioning his paid mercenaries.

"So you're the boss." I had always assumed as much but it did no harm to be sure. "You must have telephoned your friends this afternoon, immediately after I called you. You told them to follow us out to the New Territories, and when I gave you the opportunity of going back with my car you simply collected your little army and brought them in."

Slater looked at me uncertainly, but then decided that he was so definitely in control that he didn't need to get worried or angry. He simply nodded.

"You've figured it all out right, David, and somehow you knew about

Chuck and Jay. You know, you're a damned good detective."

"But not quite good enough." I said ruefully. "I still haven't figured out exactly what you want."

"I want this place," he said simply. He looked all round the working tables and the array of processing equipment and he smiled. "What I want is what I've now got — control of a major heroin factory."

"I did figure it out that far," I said apologetically. "You came to me looking for Lin Hoi, just a cheap little pusher, but you didn't really want him. He was just a starting point. Then came the late and unlamented Mr. Shing, but you didn't want him either. Neither were you interested in the Happy Valley Fruit Company or Cheng-Weng junks. They were all just stepping stones to what you really wanted. What I still don't understand, Ralph — is *why* do you want to take over a heroin factory? Surely you don't expect to set yourself up in business and make a fat profit. Maybe you can take control of what's here now and cash in this one shipment that's awaiting distribution. But that will be the end of it, Ralph. Even if May Ling's syndicate friends don't come gunning for your blood, there'll still be no more supplies of raw opium."

Slater smiled bleakly. "I don't need any more opium supplies, because I'm not planning to take over this operation on a permanent basis. All I want is the control of one bulk heroin shipment, and I'm not doing this for profit."

"How about your daughter Marion?" I suggested. "Or am I right in thinking that your daughter Marion never existed?"

He nodded slowly. "You are right. I never had a daughter. I never had a wife. I never had any kids. All I ever had was a city!" He stopped there and a strange, anguished look came over his ugly face. "I don't know if you could ever understand that, David."

I wasn't sure that I could, but then

there was a movement in the high, bolt-hole doorway set half way up the wall on the far side of the factory. Tracey Ryan appeared on the small concrete platform at the head of the flight of descending stone steps, and she answered in my place.

"Perhaps David doesn't understand — and maybe I do. You should remember, Ralph, that we come from the same city."

Slater spun round to face her, and the rest of his gang also twisted away from me with startled faces. I could have made a reach for my shoulder holster then, but I didn't. Tracey appeared calm enough, but something in her stare told me that her appearance had done nothing yet to swing the odds in my favour. In the letter that I had propped against her typewriter, I had instructed her to bring the police along if Belinda and I had not returned from the monastery in a reasonable time, but an organized police raid would not have allowed her into the firing line alone. I watched her face but saw no sign of reassurance in her emerald eyes, and so for the moment I held my hand.

There was a moment of silence and then Tracey continued:

"There's something that Ralph has not told us, David. He isn't just plain Mr. Slater, an ordinary estate agent from New York. He's Police Captain Ralph Slater of New York narcotics squad."

I was prepared for any sort of surprise, but Fletcher and Rennick were not. Their jaws hung open, and then they looked to Slater. When he didn't deny it their faces became ominous. Fletcher pushed the old monk out of his way and the little Bhikkhu tripped over the edge of his yellow robe and fell to the floor. He lay there petrified. Fletcher and Rennick shifted the aim of their Colt 0.45s so that they could cover Slater as well as myself.

"I had the feeling right from the start that I'd seen you somewhere before." Tracey was still addressing Slater. "The notion kept pestering me, and during those five days I spent in Macau I had plenty of time to work on it. I knew you came from New York, and before I teamed up with David I spent a lot of time in New York working on narcotics with the FBI. I finally convinced myself that I had seen you around one of the New York precinct stations. So I sent a cable to an old-mutual friend of ours, Police Chief MacGregor."

She paused there, she was a good story-teller and she had a captive audience. Everyone was paying attention.

"When I got back to the office this evening I found a note left by David telling me all about the Golden Light Monastery." Tracey went on. "There was also a return cable from Police Chief MacGregor. He informed me that Police Captain Slater had been one of the best cops in the business. Then, after fifteen years in the police force, and two years of working almost round the clock on New York's narcotics problem, Police Captain Slater had a mental breakdown. He flipped his lid and started taking the law into his own hands. He was suspected of starting his own Kill-a-Pusher campaign. Three known drug pedlars turned up dead with their necks broken by somebody's big hands. There was no positive proof, and maybe the New York police force didn't really want to find any, but Captain Slater was quietly dismissed from the force and recommended to take voluntary psychiatric treatment. However there's no record that he ever saw a psychiatrist. Instead, after a few months he simply disappeared from New York."

There was another silence at the end of her revelation, and then Fletcher and Rennick turned coldly towards Slater.

"Is she right," Rennick asked dangerously. "Are you a lousy cop?"

"I was a cop," Slater said harshly. "But don't let it worry you. Like the lady said they kicked me out of the police force, and now I'm just a private citizen like anyone else. I've hired you guys and I'm paying you well to do a job. The job still stands and the pay is still there to be earned. Nothing has changed."

Fletcher and Rennick looked undecided. The complications were getting beyond them.

I said quietly, "What is the job, Ralph? What do you intend to do with this one shipment of heroin?"

Slater turned slowly to look at me, and the anguish was back in his eyes. He didn't answer directly because he still wanted me to understand.

"New York was *my* city, David. It's the greatest city in America, and that means the greatest city in the whole damned world. I was born there. I grew up there. I lived there all my life. I was a cop there for fifteen years. I started out as a rookie on the beat and finally I made Police Captain. In my precinct I knew every sidewalk, every block, every back alley, every penthouse and every slum. And I knew the people. Sometimes they hated

317

cops. Sometimes they threw insults, or rotten eggs, and sometimes they even fired bullets at us, but I knew them and they knew me, and even when they were dumb enough to think they had cause to hate my guts they were still my people. They were *my* people, because they were part of *my* city. I've loved some women in my time, but maybe I didn't love them hard enough. The only thing that ever really got under my skin was New York — my City."

"You're just a natural-born cop," I said softly. "A sucker for your own little chunk of humanity."

He didn't seem to hear. He just kept on staring at me.

"Then it all began to go wrong. New York started to go down the hill. The crime rate started to go up. People blamed the cops and so they hated us more and co-operated less, and so the crime figures just got worse and worse. All the decent people started running out and the bums kept flooding in. New York got to be the kind of place where you can get fourteen murders on a peak day. The kind of place where you can't walk up a dark alley or across an open park without getting beaten up and robbed. The kind of place where people daren't let their kids out, and a woman would rather climb ten flights of stairs than risk riding in an elevator. Now nobody dares walk alone at night, and even in daylight the old and the weak have to walk in fear. That's New York! That's *my city*! It's turned sick and brutal and sunk back into the middle ages. It's worse than any kind of jungle."

He paused for breath, and then went on harshly:

"Two years ago they transferred me to the drug squad. Sure, New York's got all the big city problems, pollution, over-population, under-employment, too big a gap between Madison Avenue and the poor blacks in the Ghettos — and narcotics. Most of all narcotics. At least three-quarters of a million people in New York regularly use narcotics. The whole city stinks of drug-rotten junkies who have to lie and steal and kill, just to carry on their miserable lives. Between four and five million dollars, gets spent by New York addicts every single day on heroin alone. That's why we have such a high crime record. That's why we get all these muggings and hold-ups and stupid little murders. The junkies need money for their dope, and the only way that they can get it is through crime. It's narcotics that is New York's biggest problem. The junkies and the dope pushers are nothing but human filth who are turning my city into nothing but one great big sewer full of human rats."

He was spilling out words so fast that he was getting hoarse, but still he hadn't got to the point. I tried to help him.

"It's a big problem", I said. "But you tried to do something about that problem, Ralph. You worked on it."

"Sure," he snarled bitterly. "I worked on it, seven days a week, day and night, round the clock — for two whole damned years I worked on it. But it's out of control. There's nothing any man can do. There are too many junkies, too many pushers, too many people making big profits, and too many cops above my head taking graft. I could spend weeks making an arrest, and some smart-ass lawyer could get my man out of jail in less than an hour. I might as well have tried to piss into a hurricane!"

"So you stopped using the law, and tried your own way."

He nodded. "Sure, I killed those three pushers. I broke their rotten, stinking necks, and that was better than they deserved. But for that they booted me out of the police force. After fifteen years they just booted me out for trying to do my job in the only possible way that was left! The whole city's gone mad and they send me for psychiatric treatment!"

"But you didn't go for treatment," I said gently. "Instead you came to

Hong Kong, you came to me. You're still working on that narcotics problem. You've got another idea — a new plan. What is it, Ralph?"

He smiled, but it was a contorted smile and there was sweat on his face.

"You might as well know, David, I'm going to let this shipment go through. I reckon that in a few hours May Ling's syndicate friends will be here in force to take it back. I'll offer them a cash deal and let them buy us off cheap, or if it comes to it we'll put up a show fight and let them drive us out. Either way this shipment takes its normal course, smuggled in a million tiny little packages along its normal channels to New York. The only difference is that this shipment is going to have another ingredient mixed in at the source, before it gets divided up into all those individual little packages. I figured on strychnine, because like heroin it also has a bitter taste."

He paused, staring at me. "Can't

you see the sense of it, David? The only reason that narcotics abuse gets out of control is because the junkies protect their pushers and the others who exploit them. But feed them on a whole shipment of lethal heroin laced with strychnine and all that is going to change. A hundred thousand junkies are going to get wiped out overnight, but they are already poisoned wrecks who are better off dead anyway. Some of those who are left are going to realize how and why their buddies died, and they'll turn on their pushers. There's going to be a whole lot of human garbage left lying around in the streets to be cleared up, but at the end of it New York will be purged. My city will be clean again!"

His eyes were burning wildly and there was a trickle of spittle forming at the corner of his mouth, and I knew without any further shadow of doubt that he was insane.

18

AFTER Slater had finished there was a long silence. I had no way of knowing what kind of story and deal he had offered to his two American lieutenants, but clearly this was the first time that they had heard the truth. The faces of both Fletcher and Rennick showed surprise, and they were momentarily at a loss. Slater finally turned away from me and looked back to Tracey who was still standing on the stair-top platform half way up the far wall.

"You'd better come down here and join David and Belinda," he said slowly. "Somehow I'm going to have to hold all three of you until it's too late for any of you to stop me. I don't want to have to kill any of you, so please don't make me. You've already made one mistake by coming here alone."

"It wasn't exactly my mistake," Tracy said wryly. "And I didn't exactly come alone. I had the misfortune to get mixed up with some bad company on the way."

She moved to one side, and we all saw what she meant. The open doorway behind her slowly filled up with old army uniforms and ancient Kuomintang caps. The tall old Kuomintang General with the round face and the wisp of white beard was foremost, and flanking him on either side were his two old comrades. Two younger men brought up the rear. All of them carried Chinese machine pistols at the ready and they effectively covered the whole of the underground factory. Their faces were grim.

Slater froze, while Fletcher and Rennick had the sense to lower their gun hands slowly to point at the stone floor. May Ling pressed closer to the bars of her prison and her face was suddenly elated.

"Father!" she cried happily.

The old General looked towards her and smiled, and then the smile became a frown of anger as he saw that she was sealed behind the iron grating. He must have overheard Ralph Slater's outburst, but either he did not understand English or he was simply not interested in what Slater had had to say. He looked directly at me and spoke coldly in Cantonese.

"You are David Chan?"

I stepped forward and bowed politely. "I am."

"It was you who killed one of my young guards, on the beach where we loaded the junk *Yellow Lotus*."

I nodded sadly. "It was an unfortunate necessity."

"Father," May Ling was bewildered. "What is this all about? Why are you here?"

The old General signed to her to be patient, and continued speaking to me.

"We found the dead guard after the *Yellow Lotus* had sailed. I made

326

an investigation and interrogated every person who had been on that beach, but none of them could explain his death. We searched, and found footprints that vanished into the sea. I suspected that another vessel had followed the *Yellow Lotus*, and that someone from that other vessel had come ashore to spy, and to kill my guard. My daughter had told me the name David Chan, and how his interest had made it necessary to eliminate Mr. Shing, who was one of our representatives here in Hong Kong. I realized that there must be serious trouble here, and so when the next junk arrived to take a cargo of opium I and my comrades accompanied it on the return voyage. I ordered the junk Captain to make all possible use of his auxiliary engine, so that we arrived well ahead of schedule. I came straight to this monastery, and picked up this woman on the way. She was attempting to climb over the outer wall."

He paused there, and then commanded bluntly.

"Now you will please release my daughter."

I shrugged my shoulders as though I saw no option, and then turned to face the small cell. I smiled philosophically at May Ling, and then nodded to Belinda to pull down the locking lever set in the wall. Belinda operated the lever reluctantly while I lifted up the iron grating and pushed it above my head. Belinda released the lever into the lock position, and as she did so I caught her eye. Inside the cell, behind the jutting buttresses that formed the arched doorway, was the safest place if the bullets should start to fly, and I tried to indicate as much with a meaning glance. Belinda looked baffled and I could only hope that she would work it out for herself.

"Allow me to escort you to your father," I said as May Ling tried to push past me, and I checked her politely with my hand on her arm. She gave me a hostile glare and I added, "It is the least that I can do."

I started to lead her across the factory floor, but when I was only half way across I suddenly swung her body in front of my own and snapped a swift left arm lock around her throat. In the same moment my right hand dived inside my jacket and I pulled out the 9 mm Chinese automatic from beneath my left arm. The five threatening machine pistols jumped in alarm, but I had picked an effective shield and the old General shouted at his men to hold their fire. May Ling was already shocked into immobility and I touched the muzzle of my automatic just behind her right eye.

"Let's all be calm," I said quietly, and looking up, directly at the General. "We are now in a position to bargain, and there is no need for anyone to get hurt."

The two old soldiers had moved forward uncertainly. They kept a tight grip on their machine pistols and both weapons were pointed down at my head. They looked at their leader for advice. The old General's face had tightened with rage, but the weakening eyes beneath the peak of his cap also showed a more reassuring fear. He lowered his own machine pistol by a few inches.

"Release her, Mr. Chan," he said harshly. "Release my child, or for this you will most certainly die."

"I have no desire to harm your daughter, General," I said calmly. "But you are holding a prisoner who is equally dear to me. I will offer you a fair exchange, May Ling for Miss Ryan."

He stared down at me, and then looked to Tracey. One of his younger men had hauled her back with a machine pistol jammed in her ribs in the moment that I had made my move, but now the old man signed to him to release her. He took Tracey's arm and brought her forward.

"I could agree to an exchange," he said. "I am an old man and my daughter is all that is dear to me.

But what will happen then?"

"I would suggest that you take your daughter and your friends and retreat the way you came," I said quietly. "There is nothing more that you can do here. I left instructions for Miss Ryan to notify the police before she attempted to follow me to this monastery, and I am sure that she will have followed those instructions to the letter. At any moment now I expect the police to surround this place. Please make no mistake, this end of your operation is finished. If you delay to take a pointless vengeance then you are all lost."

"How can I know that I can trust you?"

"You have five machine pistols to my one automatic," I reminded him. "Once I release your daughter then it is I who must trust you to keep our bargain." I paused there and then took a calculated risk. "I do not think that after more than twenty years you would wear that uniform without honour. I will accept the word of a senior

Kuomintang officer."

He stared down at me, and all the dignity and pride came back into his lined face. He straightened his shoulders beneath the worn epaulettes with their rows of polished stars, and I knew that I had judged him correctly.

"You have the word of General Kang Chu-Ling," he said firmly.

"It is enough," I answered.

I lowered my automatic and released May Ling. She half turned hesitantly to look into my face. Her eyes were confused, but I smiled at her.

"You heard the bargain. You may go to your father."

Her throat moved as she swallowed her relief, and then she turned and began to walk away. I looked up expectantly at the old General and he relaxed his grip on Tracey's arm. He signed to her to go and his companions lowered their weapons to let her pass. Tracey slowly descended the stone steps to the factory floor. There she stood aside to make way for May Ling.

It was all taking place so smoothly that I had temporarily forgotten about Ralph Slater and his two armed lieutenants. I didn't think that they would be foolish enough to try anything against five machine pistols, but although I was probably right about Fletcher and Rennick, I was wrong about Slater.

"No," Slater shouted suddenly. "That crummy bastard isn't going to get away as easily as that."

I turned as he lifted his Colt 0.45, and there was nothing that I could do to stop him squeezing the trigger and blasting off a bullet. He was aiming accurately at Kang Chu-Ling, and the old General gave a sudden cry and spun sideways to crash into one of his ancient friends. The second old man pushed forward in an effort to retain his own balance, and as the General slumped down he fell away from the stair-top platform and his body dropped the vertical twelve feet to the factory floor.

I sprang forward on instinct as the

underground room was abruptly filled with gunfire. Three machine pistols opened up simultaneously and sprayed the area behind me, while the three Colt 0.45s banged off a more staccato barrage of shots. I concentrated on a racing dive that collected up both Tracey and May Ling and hurled them together to the floor. May Ling was screaming as she saw her father fall, but my weight slammed the breath and the scream right out of her lungs.

As I knocked the two girls clear I rolled over on to my back and raised up on my left elbow, the Chinese automatic ready in my right hand. I was out of sight and below the line of fire of the group of old Kuomintang soldiers in the doorway high up the wall, but another of the old men took a hit and came tumbling down almost on top of me. It seemed as though bullets were ricocheting in all directions. Slater's hired Chinese hoodlums were panicking and screaming as they scrambled to find cover or a way out. Chuck Rennick let out the most agonized screech of all, and I saw him drop his Colt and then stagger backwards to sit down hard on his backside with his hands clasping his stomach. Slater and Fletcher had found refuge behind a couple of the heavy working tables and were firing blindly.

I looked along the floor to where the old General lay out-stretched on his back. His peaked cap had rolled away and his machine pistol lay a yard from his hooked fingers. I squirmed my way towards it on my belly, reaching out with my left hand. I was almost there when Slater spotted me. He was firing rapidly at the doorway high above my head, where I guessed that the three surviving men with the machine pistols had taken refuge in the passage behind them. When I moved into his range of vision he changed his aim, cursing me, and making me his new target. His first shot kicked up a savage spray of stone chips and fragments in my face, and I didn't dare let him take a second.

I forgot the machine pistol as I drew back briefly and shot him through the heart with the Chinese automatic.

When Slater fell there was only one armed man left on the factory floor.

"Fletcher," I yelled sharply. "Drop that gun and put your hands on your head."

Jay Fletcher hesitated only briefly. The old soldiers had stopped firing when they saw Slater fall, and for the moment we were the only two figures in the drama. Fletcher's dark head was raised above the level of the table he had chosen as his refuge, and he was looking straight across the factory and into the pointing muzzle of my automatic. He made his choice and tossed his Colt out on to the factory floor. His empty hands appeared and he clasped them on top of his head.

I picked up the machine pistol with my left hand and glanced to where Tracey and May Ling were cautiously disentangling themselves.

"Tell your father's friends to continue

to hold their fire," I instructed May Ling quietly.

She hesitated, but then she looked at her father again. She blurted the necessary words of restraint in a choken voice, and then she stumbled to the old General's side.

I straightened up slowly and returned my automatic to the shoulder holster. Then I shifted the machine pistol to my right hand. Tracey was unharmed and approaching with May Ling. I searched anxiously for Belinda but it seemed that she had interpreted my last glance in good time. Her face was peeping warily but quizzically from behind the solid stone buttress that effectively screened off a protected corner of the alcove cell.

There was a movement above and I looked up. The only survivor of the ancient military trio had emerged from the doorway again and he too was searching for his fallen comrades. I made no hostile moves and we faced each other silently for a moment. Then he looked past me and the tears began to seep out of his rheumy old eyes and trickle down his wrinkled yellow face. His machine pistol slumped in his hands, and then he slung it back over one shoulder by the strap as though acknowledging that it could serve him no more. He descended the steps quickly and paused by the first of his fallen friends. However, the old soldier who had landed almost on top of me during the battle was already dead.

Kang Chu-Ling was just alive, but he was fading fast. May Ling knelt weeping by his side, while Tracey tried to comfort her. I joined them with the last old soldier.

"Well, Mr. David Chan" — the old General's dimming eyes were open, and despite the bullet lodged in his chest he was determined to speak — "what will happen now?"

"We made a bargain," I said softly. "It changes nothing that we were interrupted by a third person. You were prepared to honour your word, and I will honour mine. One of your companions is dead, but May Ling is free to leave with those who remain. I would suggest that they all return to the mainland. There is no longer any place for any of you here."

"But my father?" May Ling looked at me with real tears pouring freely down her face. "What of my father?"

I hesitated, but the old General was still capable of making his own answer.

"You will leave me here," he told her feebly. "I am a dying man. My life is measured in minutes now. I would only burden your escape."

She looked down at him and choked with grief, and painfully he shaped his last smile.

"I am dying from a bullet. That is a fitting way for an old soldier to die. This is the way that I should have died, twenty-five years ago at the head of my troops. I fought hard for China in our great civil war. It was not my wish that the Communists should win China. It was not even my wish that I should emerge from that war alive." He coughed deeply and the froth that showed between his lips was pink in colour. "It was not my wish that I should end my days smuggling opium. That is no job for a General. It was fate that trapped me in Yunnan at the end of war. It was fate that forced my path. I am thankful that fate has at least allowed me to die from a bullet."

May Ling looked up in anguish at the last old soldier.

"Uncle, we cannot leave him. We must take him with us."

"I order you to go" — Kang Chu-Ling coughed again and brought up his last word — "now."

The last old soldier looked desperately to me.

"He is right, Uncle," I said quietly. "The police will be here soon. Take May Ling and obey the General."

I heard May Ling utter a loud sob, and when I looked down again

I realized that Kang Chu-Ling was dead. There was nothing more to say and so I reached for Tracey and we both drew aside. I glanced up and saw that the two younger men who had followed the three old soldiers were now standing on the stair-top platform and watching silently. Their machine pistols were slung on their shoulders.

After a minute the old man addressed as Uncle stood up. He lifted May Ling to her feet and for another moment she wept against his chest. Then together they slowly ascended the stairs. The two younger men let them pass and then closed ranks protectively behind them. All four disappeared through the open doorway and retreated the same way that they had arrived.

★ ★ ★

When they had gone I turned at last to Tracey.

"I suppose you did notify the police?"

"Not exactly," she answered. "But I did telephone Sunny and ask him to pass the message on if he didn't hear anything from any one of us within an hour, so by that time they will be on their way."

"You should have waited for them."

"Perhaps, but I wanted to get to you first with that information on Ralph Slater. I didn't know how you would want to play it from there."

"Thanks for coming," I said. And then I took her in my arms and kissed her. I made it a long kiss, and when I released her I added: "That's just to show you that I love you."

Tracey smiled. "I love you too, David — just like a brother."

Her green eyes laughed, and I realized that at some time she and Belinda had compared notes and reached a mutual agreement on our joint relationships. Their decision, I had to concede, was right.

I slung the machine pistol over my shoulder and put my right arm around

Tracey's waist. We walked back across the factory to where Belinda waited, and I slipped my left arm around Belinda's waist. They were both a comfortable fit.

"I love you both," I said, and they both smiled.

* * *

Belinda had already picked up Slater's Colt to cover Fletcher and the surviving Chinese from Slater's gang, and so there was nothing to do except wait for the police to arrive. In the meantime I gazed regretfully at Slater himself, and brooded on the big city drug problem that had beat down an over-conscientious cop until it broke his heart and broke his mind. Ralph Slater had planned what would have been one of the biggest mass murders ever. Now it wouldn't happen, but now I was asking myself a question that I couldn't answer. Was Slater right?

Other titles in the Linford Mystery Library:

A GENTEEL LITTLE MURDER
Philip Daniels

Gilbert had a long-cherished plan to murder his wife. When the polished Edward entered the scene Gilbert's attitude was suddenly changed.

DEATH AT THE WEDDING
Madelaine Duke

Dr. Norah North's search for a killer takes her from a wedding to a private hospital.

MURDER FIRST CLASS
Ron Ellis

Will Detective Chief Inspector Glass find the Post Office robbers before the Executioner gets to them?

A FOOT IN THE GRAVE
Bruce Marshall

About to be imprisoned and tortured in Buenos Aires, John Smith escapes, only to become involved in an aeroplane hijacking.

DEAD TROUBLE
Martin Carroll

Trespassing brought Jennifer Denning more than she bargained for. She was totally unprepared for the violence which was to lie in her path.

HOURS TO KILL
Ursula Curtiss

Margaret went to New Mexico to look after her sick sister's rented house and felt a sharp edge of fear when the absent landlady arrived.

THE DEATH OF ABBE DIDIER
Richard Grayson

Inspector Gautier of the Sûreté investigates three crimes which are strangely connected.

NIGHTMARE TIME
Hugh Pentecost

Have the missing major and his wife met with foul play somewhere in the Beaumont Hotel, or is their disappearance a carefully planned step in an act of treason?

BLOOD WILL OUT
Margaret Carr

Why was the manor house so oddly familiar to Elinor Howard? Who would have guessed that a Sunday School outing could lead to murder?